T0065211

MURDER
ON THE
STREET OF
YEARS

MARC D. HASBROUCK

iUniverse

MURDER ON THE STREET OF YEARS

iUniverse books may be ordered through booksellers or by contacting:

iUniverse
1663 Liberty Drive
Bloomington, IN 47403
www.iuniverse.com
844-349-9409

ISBN: 978-1-6632-2773-7 (sc)
ISBN: 978-1-6632-2774-4 (e)

Library of Congress Control Number: 2021917220

Print information available on the last page.

iUniverse rev. date: 08/25/2021

This Book is Dedicated to all the Brave Men & Women
Who Fought in World War II

With Special Mention For These Two Men in Particular:

Carlton Joseph Hasbrouck
(My Stepfather)
Wounded in Battle: Purple Heart Recipient
World War II

2nd Lt. William R. Bennett, Jr.
(My Wife's Uncle)
He Made the Ultimate Sacrifice
Posthumously Awarded the Purple Heart
and the Air Medal with two Oak Leaf Clusters
World War II

"What's past is prologue."
William Shakespeare – The Tempest

PREFACE

"One Cannot Plan For The Unexpected."
Aaron Klug

I created a challenge for myself. In the final third of my last book, *Down With The Sun*, I wrote about an unseen, but pivotal fictional character, Victoria Brecklyn. She was a best-selling author of murder mystery novels who lived in London and wrote her books from the early 1950s into the 1980s. Under the pen name of Vicky Jayne, her popular series drew the attention of the main character in my book, Baxter Janus, and he decided to purchase a few. Being an avid reader of thrillers, he was hooked from the very first page.

If you have not yet read *Down With The Sun*, don't worry. There is no need for the enjoyment of this book. There are no connections. But the challenge I created for myself took me by surprise. I had written that Vicky Jayne, ne Victoria Brecklyn, included bits and pieces of history throughout her mysteries. She wrote about London in the years following World War II. With that in mind, and with a new book churning in my imagination just waiting to be written, I decided to write *this* book, *Murder on the Street of Years*, as the author Vicky Jayne might have. In *her* style.

London is not unfamiliar to me. It's one of my favorite cities. But London of 1952 was a different matter. Manners and mores were much different than they are these days. My challenge was to make my new book realistic (as realistic as thrillers might be) regarding culture, attire, automobiles, and locales. To create a thriller that was taking place long before the Internet and cell phones opened up the opportunities for some suspenseful scenes.

Multiple murders lie ahead on the pages that follow. You, the reader, will be challenged with *this* conundrum: can murder ever be justified?

MURDER
ON THE
STREET OF
YEARS

A Vicky Jayne Murder Mystery

*Murder is always a mistake. One should never do
anything that one cannot talk about after dinner.*
                                        Oscar Wilde

1

London, November 6, 1952

It was apparent that the body was quite dead, not merely because of the listless manner in which it was sprawled across the ground, arms and legs akimbo, but by the fact that it was also headless.

2

Two Months Earlier

With typical British resilience and resolve, England had quickly rebounded from the ravages of World War II. Granted, there were still some bombed out, vacant, or severely damaged buildings scattered throughout London, but the suburbs hummed with vibrancy. It was a period of optimism and hope. The rebuilding of the capital was remarkable, to say the least. And with the rebuilding of commerce came increased earnings and with that came an increase in culture. It was becoming a different London than before.

But certain aspects of the recently ended war persisted. Heinous aspects. Deadly aspects.

It was one of those rare cloudless, crisp mornings in early September, and autumn was in the air. Devon Stone stepped out onto the smallish front porch of his house on Carlingford Road in Hampstead to pick up the delivered morning newspaper. He inhaled the fresh air deeply, closing his eyes as he did so. *Today was going to be a good day*, he thought.

This was considered a very affluent, posh section of London and his house was what was called a Victorian Family Home, although he was the only family member. A member of one. A confirmed bachelor. The houses on the street, all of them similar, were attached side-by-side, narrow in width but deep in length and reached up three stories. Size-wise, they measured 2815 square feet, had three reception rooms, one on each floor, a decent sized kitchen with eat-in dining area, five bedrooms, three bathrooms, front and rear gardens (one being on the roof), gated off-street parking, and had fabulous views. The rooms on the main floor had higher ceilings than on the upper two floors and with elegant wainscoting on the walls. His décor was not ostentatious, more simple and modern, with many pieces of contemporary artwork on every wall, including an early Picasso and a late Kandinsky. His attention-getting furniture bore the signature designs of the likes of Mies van der Rohe, Charles Eames, Marcel Breuer and, just for the fun and whimsy of it, the fabled Butterfly Chair. Quite often inebriated guests would need help getting up and out of that one. The house was located a few short blocks from the sprawling Hampstead Heath and, what was even better, he was within easy walking distance to The Holly Bush, his favorite pub.

One might ask: *"Why five bedrooms for a bachelor?"* He entertained. A lot.

Strikingly handsome and suave in a Cary Grant kind of way, 46 years old, with sandy brown hair that was always in place, and deep blue eyes, he stood slightly over six feet tall. He had a commanding voice, an enviable vocabulary, and a memory that was frightening and unfailing in its amazing accuracy. His dear friend, and fellow mystery writer, Agatha Christie spent the war years living just a few blocks from him in what was billed as the safest building in London. He delighted in telling his friends that Christie had endured the Blitz with a pillow over her head to drown out the noise, wrapped in her prized fur coat and continued to write. A play she had written not too long after that was due to open on the West End sometime in November. Something called *The Mousetrap.*

While downplaying it in his official literary biography, during the war he worked for Britain's Naval Intelligence Division, and was involved in the planning of two intelligence units. He would interweave these activities from time to time in his novels. He maintained very close contact with his former associates in MI6, calling upon them occasionally to verify certain facts or to run potential plot points by them to quell any inaccuracies.

His prowess in the martial arts was formidable; although very few of his acquaintances were aware of it. But he used it when absolutely necessary, surprising those who were the recipients.

His latest best seller, *The Fallen*, had ignited a firestorm amongst the critics, with both praise for its extremely brazen, somewhat approving theme of revenge and strong condemnation for the exact same reason. The book asked the question: can murder ever be justified? The avalanche of fan mail that ensued fell more into the praise camp, with a smattering of hate mail for which the author kept a separate file.

With the morning newspaper tucked under his arm and a cup of steaming hot coffee in hand, he climbed the three flights to reach his rooftop garden. He opened the door and stepped out into his own private botanical paradise. Small trees and shrubs of various types – the ones that would withstand the British weather patterns—and perennials that were in full bloom greeted his sight. The pea-sized pebble gravel rooftop had been covered, in various places, with raised dirt-filled garden boxes. A waist-high wall surrounded the rooftop and abutted against the other waist-high walls of rooftops from house to house down the street. A small table with two chairs located in the center of all this beauty was his intended destination as he ambled along. He spotted his neighbor to the south out on his rooftop attending to his flock of homing pigeons in their large aviary.

"Good morning, Chester," he called out with a wave of his hand. His friend responded in kind and went on about his business.

Devon Stone sat at the table, sipped his coffee, and started to read the morning paper. A gentle breeze ruffled the edges of his *Daily Express* as he flipped through the pages. *Any new murders to report?* he thought, and chuckled to himself.

No new murders reported, but a Missing Persons notice caught his eye. He read it as he sipped his coffee once again. He leaned back in the chair with a very satisfied look on his face.

A week earlier he had nodded goodnight to his favorite barman at his favorite pub when the place was closing for the evening. He was the last to leave as he stepped out into the dark, quiet street and began slowly walking home. A few moments later he sensed that someone had emerged from behind a stand of trees and was following him. It was not unexpected. He was almost certain he knew whom. He was *positive* he knew why. Devon began taking a more circuitous route back to his house, and purposely headed down a street that was even darker and less traveled. He feigned drunkenness, stumbling and weaving from side to side. The old sidewalk was uneven, making his ruse look plausible. He started singing a rowdy little song, purposely slurring his words and giggling to himself. He waited until he reached a particularly darkened area and leaned up against a post, as if he might be ill. His follower took advantage of this seemingly intoxicated target and rushed forward.

Devon waited.

The man was within inches when Devon suddenly swirled around, lifting his right leg as high as possible, using the strongest muscles of the thigh and buttocks, lunging forward, bringing his foot down with a crushing blow on the man's foot. The attacker buckled briefly, enough time for Devon to bring his foot down again, this time on the man's calf, tearing the ligaments and spraining the knee joint. The now-whimpering man fell to the ground in agony and surprise, dropping the knife he had intended to use on Devon's throat. Devon Stone bent down holding the man's jacket by the collar and flipped him onto his back while straddling him. He quickly shifted both strong hands to grip the man's neck and squeezed, pressing his thumbs into the man's trachea. He got *his* face so close to the attacker's face that he could smell tobacco mixed with a trace of whiskey on the struggling man's breath. And his breathing was slowly becoming more difficult. He got his face even closer as the man's eyes began to bulge. The man tried to struggle and fight but his arms were somewhat restricted by his position and Devon outweighed him by at least one stone. He was beginning to weaken and Devon could feel the man's muscles as they relaxed, giving in. Giving up.

"Hello, Freddy," Devon said with a smile and a wink. "Goodbye,

Freddy," he said as he heard the man's cricoid cartilage crack and the eyes suddenly became vacant.

"Oh, blast, and these were new trousers, too," Devon said as he glanced at a newly torn hole in his knee.

Looking around quickly to make sure no one saw the action, no matter how swiftly it had occurred, he then dragged the unsuccessful assassin further into the bushes and trees, unable to be seen from the street should anyone happen to pass by. He ran the few blocks to his house, went to the gated parking area, and retrieved his car. Driving it to the scene of his attack, he got out, again making sure no one was around. He opened the car's boot, carried the lifeless body from its hiding place and carefully laid it inside. Throwing the man's knife in there as well, he closed the compartment, got back into his brand new Armstrong Siddeley Sapphire and slowly drove off into the night. Ironically, the crystal clear voice of the beloved Vera Lynn was singing *Auf Wiederseh'n Sweetheart* on the car radio. He whistled along with the tune.

•

Two houses to the north of Devon's lived an eighty-year-old widow, Mildred Wallace. Decades earlier a young nephew of hers couldn't pronounce Mildred, calling her Min instead. Being that she was just barely over five feet tall, from that time on even her closest friends, and she had many, lovingly called her Little Min. During the war, she was rushing through her house to find shelter from an air raid when she slipped on the waxed hardwood flooring, losing her footing on a small scatter rug, falling and severely breaking her left leg. Not being able to receive prompt attention and then getting shoddy surgery when she did, she now walked with a very pronounced limp, not being able to bend her leg at the knee. She looked years younger than eighty, acted even younger and enjoyed gin. A lot. More often than not, she slept until noon but today seemed different for some reason. She was up and about by nine, went out to her back terrace drawing her robe around her waist and inhaled the crisp morning air, closing her eyes as she did so. *Today was going to be a good day*, she thought.

She loved flowers and had several potted geraniums in full bloom. She bent over by one, rubbing a leaf between her fingers then smelling the aroma on her fingertips. She found that a refreshing fragrance. She also enjoyed the fragrance of marigolds, of which she had half dozen more pots of various sizes. Although she, too, could have a rooftop garden, her severe limp prevented her from climbing all those stairs. She did so only on rare occasions. For the most part, the top two floors of her house were seldom visited except by her cleaning service from time to time or overnight guests.

Her late husband had been an extremely important player in Britain's Secret Intelligence Service, the SIS, which eventually became Military Intelligence, Section 6—otherwise known as MI6. Although he had died under bewildering circumstances years earlier, Little Min was convinced to this day that the Germans were involved somehow.

She brewed herself some Black tea, and then returned to her back yard terrace and the small wisteria-covered gazebo in the center. She sipped her first cup of the day as she casually thumbed through the morning paper. A particular item caught her attention. A Missing Persons notice. She lifted the cup to her lips once more as a satisfied smile crept across her face.

•

Two houses to the south of Devon's lived Mildred Winsom. Millie to her friends, although she had very few, was raven-haired, rail-thin, tall, and had the demeanor of a cornered feral cat. Divorced twice before she reached the age of thirty-five, now 40, she was keeping company, *very* discretely, with a married man five years her senior. She grew a large flower and vegetable garden on her rooftop terrace, enjoying vine-ripened tomatoes during the summer months and canning a vast amount for the winter. Intoxicating aromas would quite often waft from her open windows at dinner times throughout the warm months. She loved to cook. A lot. She unlocked her front door to retrieve the morning newspaper from the top step, inhaling the crisp air as she did so. She wrinkled up her nose; cautiously looking up and down the street in both directions before ducking quickly back inside, relocking the door. *Today was going to be a lousy day,* she thought. *Another one.*

With a cup of coffee and the morning paper in hand she sat at her kitchen table, trepidation surged through her as to what she might discover when she started reading. It had been this way for the past week. It was giving her a headache. Finally, the notice she had dreaded was there. *Another one gone,* she thought to herself, *they're getting closer.*

She stood up abruptly and crumpled the tabloid into a tight ball and threw it as hard as she could at the kitchen wall knocking a picture askew. She sat down again abruptly and seethed. She pounded the table so hard with her fist that it sent her coffee cup onto the floor where it shattered.

Little Min, Devon, and Millie started their days. Before the sun comes up tomorrow, one of them will be dead. Murdered.

3

Billy Bennett rolled over in bed, reaching for his pack of Lucky Strike that was on his hotel nightstand. He lit his cigarette, drawing in deeply, holding it for a moment and then exhaling the smoke through his nose. He closed his eyes and envisioned himself flying through the skies, conducting bombing runs over Germany. Now discharged from the army, with the war long since over, he sometimes longed for the fight once again. The adrenaline pumping, the thrill, the victory. The good-versus-evil thing. Quite often his nightly dreams consisted of just that.

He actually had no *real* desire to return to active duty. He felt that at the ripe old age of nearly 34 he was too old. His country was going through a period that the press had dubbed "America's Winter of Discontent", with most citizens being frustrated by the stalemate of the on-going Korean War. Billy was more or less blasé about *that* conflict and was hoping that a new administration in Washington would soon resolve the issue. But he pushed all those thoughts aside. He was here in London for a week of fun and a bit of relaxation. A little bit of romance wouldn't hurt, either.

After being severely wounded during battle and receiving a Purple Heart medal as a result, he had returned home to the United States, to his hometown in New Jersey, but he had recently flown back to London for a short visit with the beautiful young lady he had met during the war. Veronica Barron, Ronnie to Billy, was an American singer/actress who was

one of the many performers in the United Service Organizations, otherwise
known as the USO. Following the invasion of Normandy, the American
actor Edward G. Robinson was the first movie star to travel to Normandy
to entertain the troops. Many others soon followed. Billy met Ronnie when
she performed with the USO at a little local theater somewhere in France.
There was an immediate spark between the two, and they met for drinks
a few times after her show, which led to late-night dinners beyond that.
And even more beyond that.

Billy was a handsome rogue. Ronnie had teasingly called him that
after a couple dinner dates following his discharge from the army. A
stylish, dapper dresser, he always wore a suit or sports jacket and necktie
out in public and, recently, with the current rage for men, an addition
of a narrow-brimmed Trilby hat. His jaunty hat was *always* worn at the
rakish angle of 10° from horizontal. Because of his military background,
he almost constantly appeared to be standing at attention. And, at six
feet-two in height, he surely stood out amongst most of the shorter Brits.
Dark brown hair with reddish highlights and intense brown eyes made the
ladies swoon. He was not oblivious to that reaction but, although he was
flattered and, at times, acted a bit cocky, he was also surprisingly modest.

He stubbed out his cigarette and, still in his pajamas, flipped through
his small address book to find a telephone number. Picking up the phone
on his nightstand, he asked the hotel operator to place the call. Glancing
at his watch he realized that he had slept practically all day. It was almost
quarter to four. No wonder he was so hungry.

"Hi, toots, it's me, Billy," he said excitedly as he recognized Veronica's
melodious voice when she answered. "My plane got in very late last night,
or rather very early this morning after a couple delays and detours. I had
to get some shut-eye before I collapsed. I can't wait to see you again, but I
know you'll be at the theater soon for your show," he said as he glanced at
his wristwatch once again. "Can we meet afterwards at a pub or something
for some drinks and dinner? Gosh, I miss you *so* much!"

Veronica laughed. "Hey, slow down, cowboy, and catch your breath.
I'm eager to see you, too, sweetheart. Hello, by the way," and she giggled.

"I have a much better plan and it won't cost you a plug nickel. Well, except for cab fare. Yes, I'll be heading out to the theater in a few minutes. Get yourself freshened up and head there, too. I always get two house seats for every performance and a ticket will be there at the box office with your name on it tonight. My roommate has a very good friend, a Devon something or other, who is throwing one of his many parties tonight and we're all invited. So, after the show we can get reacquainted there. Oh, you probably don't know but the pubs all close here at ten every night, so they'd be closed after the show ended anyway. And, also, in case you didn't know, the theater is the Drury Lane. Your cabbie will know where it is. No problem with that!"

They chatted for a few more minutes before Veronica had to make her exit and head to the theater. Billy hastily threw off his pajamas and took a long, lingering hot bath, leaning back in the tub with his second cigarette of the day dangling from his lips. Occasionally an ash would fall into the water as he soaked and smoked but he never noticed.

He smiled to himself as the memories of this beautiful woman swirled through his mind. Although Veronica was American, she had lived in London since the end of the war. Billy wished that she had decided to return to the States to live, but he knew that she had found work easily because of her great talent and even greater beauty. He was proud of the fact that she had apparently fallen in love with him despite the distance. But she loved the London theater scene and it loved her right back. Starring in both musicals and comedies, her audiences could count on consistently great performances, rewarding her with thunderous applause. Although he had yet to meet her roommate, he knew that Veronica shared a small, but efficient two-bedroom flat with another young lady named Alexis Morgan. The two women had struck up a conversation at the Lamb & Flag, a venerable old pub in Covent Garden where Alexis worked as a barmaid. It was within walking distance to the theater where Veronica now starred. They had hit it off immediately and became instant friends. Veronica was so likeable and, as Billy almost sang to himself as he thought about her, *You'd be so easy to love...*

Billy stepped from the tub still humming the song, dried off, and then wrapped the towel around his trim waist as he shaved. By the time he had gotten dressed, the pot of steaming hot coffee he had ordered from room service was at his door.

•

It was a matter of semantics, but to say that Clovis James was ugly would be a gross understatement. However, it wasn't because of his appearance. On the contrary. He was actually a very good-looking gentleman. His wavy dark blond hair, dimpled chin, and sparkling blue eyes were alluring, especially to young ladies when they first saw him. But once they chatted with him for even a short moment, the entrancement ended swiftly. Appearing older than his 48 years, he always seemed to be unhappy for one reason or another. He couldn't remember when he last felt joy. Consequently, he would find fault with everything and, worse, with everyone. No matter whom he was with, or what they might be doing, Clovis would criticize. It was never a mild critique, at that. He was cruel and sarcastic. He was paid, and handsomely, to critique. He was the theater critic for *The Guardian,* a newspaper dating back to 1821. Several thespians of both genders that had been on the receiving end of his barbs throughout the years were convinced that he was present when the paper first went to press.

He was putting the finishing touches on a column he was writing for the Sunday edition, comparing the current London season to the Broadway season. Returning from New York less than a week before, he had been extremely impressed by José Ferrer in *The Shrike,* hoping that both he and the play would make it to the West End. The play was what some might call a psychological thriller and it left the audiences on edge even after the final moments and the curtain had come down. He pushed back from his typewriter as his telephone rang.

"I was wondering when you might be calling," he said, with a wry grin. "Yes. Yes, of course I heard. Well, actually I *read* about it this morning. Doesn't happen to me very often, as you know, but it put a smile on my face. The numbers *are* dwindling. We're making progress. Not quickly enough, but nonetheless. I'm sure the rest of them might be getting a bit nervous about now. Or desperate."

He listened to his caller further, nodding to himself.

"Yes, that name sounds *somewhat* familiar but I can't be sure if our information is accurate. We need concrete verification."

He listened further, leaning forward, phone receiver tucked between his ear and shoulder, to correct a typographical error he spotted in his column. He pursed his lips.

"Alright, I'll be there this evening. But I really want to stay out of sight. Someone near and dear to us, I say with tongue planted firmly in cheek, may have some suspicions about my recent activities. I need to be coy."

The phone call ended and he finished his column.

•

Gregory Montgomery stepped from a late afternoon bath and, standing naked, looked at himself in the mirror. No, actually he *smiled* at himself in the mirror. He turned this way then that, admiring his muscled body. *Not bad for 38*, he thought, *not bad at all*. He flexed his right bicep, then his left. Then both of them at the same time. He was often referred to as a better-looking, better-built David Niven by many of his reviewers. He was an actor and had just gotten rave reviews (well, except from *one* critic) for his performance in the hit revival of Noel Coward's *Private Lives* at the Drury Lane. His costar, Veronica Barron, had also gotten rave reviews and Gregory was hoping that soon she would be another one of his many conquests. The fact that his conquests, no matter how discrete, often consisted of either gender didn't go unnoticed by a perceptive, persistent, prying theater critic.

Gregory Montgomery concealed another, far more dangerous and deadly secret from his adoring fans.

The telephone rang, breaking the spell that was happening between Gregory and his reflection. He glanced at his watch. *Almost time to head off to the theater anyway*, he thought to himself.

Before he even had a chance to say hello, an agitated voice announced, "I think she's a witch. She's one of them. I thought she was dead."

"Wait. Who? What are you talking about?"

"There's someone at the door. I'll ring you right back."

He waited as long as he could, but no return call ever came.

Billy, Clovis and Gregory headed out into the world to do what they do best. Before the year's end, one of them would be dead. Murdered.

4

Mildred Winsom had just begun a hastily made phone call when the doorbell rang. Although she was not expecting anyone, she ended her call abruptly and went down her front hall to the door. Her dinner was already getting cold and would soon get colder. She saw a silhouette through the stained glass windows of her front door but couldn't make it out as either male or female. She unlocked the door and cautiously opened it a crack. She stepped back and her eyes widened in surprise, then narrowed in hatred. She stepped further back.

"What are *you* doing here? More to the point, how did you find me?"

The front door was pushed closed.

The applause was still ringing in her ears when Veronica rushed into Billy's arms, unabashedly kissing him squarely on the lips. He had been waiting by the stage door but had been ushered back into the theater and then backstage by a fellow cast member sent by Veronica. Her vivid red stage makeup lipstick instantly transferred to Billy's lips and sent her into fits of laughter.

"What?" Billy asked, unawares, throwing up his arms. "Was that a lousy kiss or what? I thought it was pretty darn good! What's so funny?"

She turned him around so he could see himself in a nearby mirror. He simply smirked and shrugged his shoulders. He took out a handkerchief, quickly wiping his lips.

"You were amazing," Billy gushed. "I can't remember when I've laughed so much. Ronnie, you were born to play that part. Gosh, you look great!"

Veronica Barron had the look that could stop traffic and often did. At 32, and standing a demure 5'4", she had long, wavy blonde hair that swooped down over her right eye from time to time. Her fans called it her peek-a-boo look. She had the lithe body of a dancer and always moved with grace.

Amid all the hubbub backstage, Billy suddenly felt another presence close behind him. He turned too quickly and came face-to-face, and much too closely at that, with a handsome man still in his stage makeup.

"And who might *you* be?" asked Gregory Montgomery, almost with a sneer.

"Gregory, please meet my *very* dear friend Billy Bennett. He's flown all the way from America just to visit with me. He adored the play, by the way."

"Greg, it's a pleasure meeting you," Billy said, smiling broadly while extending his hand. "Your performance was top notch. Oh, can I call you Greg?"

"No. I've never in my life gone as Greg. It's always been Gregory. The pleasure is all mine," he said coldly as he turned and walked away, ignoring Billy's outstretched hand.

Billy felt a bit embarrassed but Veronica brushed it off. She turned her head to see if anyone else would be in hearing distance. She leaned into Billy and whispered into his ear.

"Gregory is jealous, I can tell. He's known in certain circles as a bit of a rake and I think he's trying to make some moves on me. If the truth were known, be careful, he might also try to make some moves on *you* as well. Please do *not* mention that to anyone else. I'll just *die* if that gets out that I spread *that* around," and then she giggled. "Let me change real quick and we'll be off to that party. It's probably just getting started if I can believe anything that my roommate tells me. Oh, and there she is!" Veronica rushed to greet her young friend, turning to introduce her to Billy.

Alexis Morgan was a statuesque beauty. Although she was almost 31, she had the kind of face that could look older, or younger, depending upon her attire and behavior. Nearly six feet tall, she had closely-cropped black hair, sparkling emerald green eyes, and a naturally beautiful face even without makeup, which she rarely wore. She was always in slacks of some fashion, tight in the waist and full in the leg. Her blouses were usually unbuttoned just enough to show off her cleavage and would be unbuttoned a bit further as the nights progressed ensuring bigger tips from her not-so-sober patrons. Her shoes were always sensible and comfortable lace-ups, considering that she spent so much time on her feet running tables at the pub.

"Wow, how lucky is *this*?" Billy grinned. "Going to a fancy party with two of the prettiest ladies in town. If I remember correctly your name is Alexis, right?" he asked, extending his hand. This time his hand was firmly grasped accompanied by a wide, friendly smile.

"Exactly right, Billy," she answered. "Alexis Morgan. I have been so eager to make your acquaintance. Veronica has told me so much about you. And meeting you, now, I'm a bit jealous. She underplayed your handsomeness."

A bit of a flirt, aren't you, young lady, thought Billy with a roguish grin. He also thought that there was something a bit disconcerting about her accent. Perhaps it was just because she and her accent might be from a different part of England. Her elocution was precise but perhaps a bit too precise. A little too studied.

"Let's go!" Veronica squealed as she stepped out of her dressing room wearing a vivid red, form-fitting pencil skirt and a white silk blouse. She stopped briefly in front of a full-length mirror to make certain her stocking seams were straight.

"Holy cow!" exclaimed Billy "You look dangerous!" And they all laughed.

•

The party was in full swing by the time their cabbie deposited them at the doorsteps of Devon Stone. The house was ablaze with light, as music seemed to tumble out of every window. People could be seen up on what was obviously a rooftop terrace.

"You're just going to love Devon," gushed Alexis. "He is so suave and knows everybody, and I mean everybody, in town."

They rushed up the twelve steps to his front door which stood wide open almost welcoming them, or anyone else, for that matter, into the swing and sway of a jazzy tempo. A short, slender, very dark-skinned man was playing a trumpet surrounded by a trio of other players.

Alexis leaned into her companions and whispered, "I've met him before, at other parties. His name is Miles something or other, I can't remember. I think he's recorded stuff back in the States. He's really good, isn't he?" They had to agree.

They stepped from the foyer into a long hallway leading to the back of the house. The oak hardwood flooring had been dark-stained and polished almost to a mirror finish. To the left was a large reception room, filled with guests. And artwork. Colorful paintings of various sizes were hung on two of the white walls above the wainscoting. The wall to the front of the house was, basically, one large ceiling to floor window covered with long dark red drapes. The fourth wall, backing up to the hallway, contained a built-in bookcase, crammed with books of all shapes and sizes. Several first editions were among the collection. The room had deep, plush steel gray carpet that one would almost sink into. A suave, dapper-looking gentleman was holding court in the center of the room. Alexis spotted him right away.

"Oh, there he is. There's Devon! Come on, I'll introduce you."

Introductions were made, with the tuxedo-wearing host kissing the ladies on both cheeks and firmly shaking Billy's hand. It was actually difficult hearing anyone speak because there was so much cacophony throughout his expansive house packed with talking, laughing fun-loving people. The trumpeter in the front entry hit an especially high note, holding it for a long, long time. Devon jokingly put his fingers into his ears and laughed. With his head he nodded to one of the other reception rooms off the side of the front hall and mouthed "The bar. In there. Drink up!"

The bar was, indeed, "in there", which the three of them discovered with pleasure. There was a very active, and obviously popular barman making the drinks as fast as the guests could down them. Billy turned with his Scotch and soda in hand, nearly knocking over a short elderly lady with a pronounced limp, causing her to drop the drink that she was holding. She was wearing a full-length emerald green silk dress with an elegant, brightly colored scarf tied around her neck, and a small black pillbox hat on her head. She had been drinking what appeared to be a martini.

"Oh, my goodness," he exclaimed in alarm. "I am so terribly sorry. I really need to be more careful, considering I haven't even had one sip yet!"

He bent down; picking up her now-empty glass, glad that it hadn't shattered when hitting the heavily carpeted floor. He dabbed at the wet floor with the paper napkin he had been handed by the barman with his drink.

"Oh, bosh, don't worry about it young man. I shouldn't be lollygagging behind handsome young men such as yourself." She extended her hand. "I'm Mildred Wallace but everyone calls me Little Min. Please do the same."

"Okay then Little Min, let me get you another drink. I feel terrible. Was that a martini you were drinking?"

"Well, yes, in a manner of speaking I suppose so," she answered with a smile.

"What do you mean by *that*? I don't understand."

Little Min laughed.

"I have the barman make them *exceptionally* dry."

"How does one do that?" Billy asked, a bit confused.

"I have him eliminate the vermouth. And no olive. It takes up too much room in the glass."

They both laughed then. Billy turned toward the barman who was prepared. He had seen the accidental spill and knew Little Min from previous parties. He handed a new, *exceptionally* dry martini to Billy who, in turn, handed it to the diminutive guest.

"Oh, heavens, I know *you*!" Little Min exclaimed as she watched

Veronica come up behind Billy. "I saw you at the Drury Lane last week. You, my dear, are just fabulous. Fabulous."

Veronica blushed. A smiling Alexis came up behind Billy with a drink in her hand as well.

"And that costar of yours, Gregory Montgomery. Well now, he's just something else, isn't he?" as she winked at them. Neither of them was quite sure what she really meant by that. "If you kids are hungry, our gracious host has a veritable feast going on in the kitchen down that way," as she pointed down the long hallway running toward the back of the house. "Devon certainly knows how to have a party. Especially when his royalties keep rolling in. Have fun kids." She turned to go, giving Alexis a little smile and a nod.

Eventually a few more of the guests began to recognize Veronica. Some would nod politely and smile, apparently either too shy or not wanting to encroach upon her private time. A few others weren't that shy. Or polite.

"Oh, my goodness gracious," gushed one older, none too slender lady as she came rushing toward both Billy and Veronica. "We just left the theater a few hours ago and, look, here you are! And is this your handsome husband?" she asked, referring to Billy, looking him up and down.

Billy opened his mouth to speak but Veronica answered.

"No, no, he's a very good friend. A *very* good friend, indeed."

"And a very proud friend, at that," interjected Billy. "*Very* proud."

He slowly backed away, not wanting to interrupt any further gushing.

"And, oh my goodness, your costumes in the show were simply divine," the woman continued, now almost ignoring Billy, and clutching her pearls. "I nearly *swooned* when you came out in that fabulous purple gown in act two. I'd give my right leg to get into that gown!"

The woman's balding husband leaned close to Billy and whispered, sotto voce, into his ear.

"Who's she fooling?" he said, "She couldn't even fit into that gown with or without her right leg!"

Billy frowned mockingly, shook his head and wagged his finger at the man.

As soon as *that* couple left Veronica's side, another one approached. The woman, elegantly dressed in a full-length shimmering black satin gown, extended her hand to Veronica, leaning in and kissing her on both cheeks. Her tuxedo-clad escort stood back smiling.

"Exquisite performance," the woman practically cooed. "I loved it so much I may have to see it again. Truly wonderful. Or maybe I should say *Wunderbar*," she said, with a sly wink thinking perhaps that she was being oh-so-clever, "because I also simply *adored* you last year in *Kiss Me, Kate*. Divine voice. Simply *wunderbar*," she repeated, almost singing the tune.

Veronica simply smiled and nodded as she backed away, turning and rejoining Billy and Alexis.

"Wow," he said, "You didn't tell me. I didn't know you were in *Kiss Me, Kate* last year."

"I wasn't. That wasn't me. It was Patricia Morison."

Alexis snickered.

The three of them were about to check out the food situation when, from across the room, Devon caught Alexis's eye, motioned to her, and moved toward a closed door off the large reception room.

"Hey, go check out the food in the kitchen. I'll catch up with you shortly," Alexis told them, as she followed Devon into the room, closing the door behind her.

"Hmmm, I wonder how well your sweet roommate knows Devon?" Billy snickered.

A few seconds later, Little Min went up to that same door, looked around, tapped lightly on it, and then went in.

"Well, well, well. The plot thickens, doesn't it?" laughed Veronica.

They slowly made their way through the crowded hallway into the kitchen where tuxedo-clad servers were dicing fresh fruits, slicing various meats, both hot and cold, and cutting up dozens of different kinds of cheeses.

"Holy cow, I never knew there were so many kinds of cheese. I just know Swiss and cheddar, oh, and Velveeta," exclaimed Billy as he surveyed the platters in front of him. "What's *that* one?" he asked a server as he pointed to a small round mound of white cheese on a small plate. He leaned in closer to look at it.

The server smiled and took a small knife, cutting off a tiny sliver.

"Here," she said, "Try it. It's not very well known. It's called Manur. It comes from unpasteurized cow's milk. From Serbia. I just now put this one out. Mr. Stone likes it very much but he doesn't have very much of it at the moment, so we usually wait until late in his parties to put this out for his guests."

"Excuse me?" Billy said, leaning in closer to the server. Perhaps he hadn't heard her correctly. "Did you just say manure? You know, like in horse poop or something?"

The server laughed and Veronica giggled.

"No, nothing like that, sir, but I really *did* say Manur, m-a-n-u-r, although some people also call it Mandur. Go ahead, sir, give it a try."

Billy took a bite, wrinkled his nose, and passed the rest of the sliver to Veronica.

"Here, Ronnie, give this one a try. It's a bit too salty for my tastes. But I can't get that name out of my mind. I think I might just stick with Swiss and cheddar."

They filled their plates with the slices of cold meats and a few chunks of cheese, avoiding the Manur, and headed up the stairs to see what was going on up on the rooftop terrace. Another young couple passed them heading back downstairs.

"It's all yours, buddy," smiled the man in passing. "Have fun," he said as he winked at Billy.

Stepping out onto the terrace, which appeared to be more of a botanical garden, they both glanced up at the cloudless sky and a brilliant crescent moon. They put their plates down on the edge of the short wall surrounding the roof.

"Gorgeous, isn't it?" Veronica sighed. "Is it waxing or waning? I can never remember which is which."

"Beats me," answered Billy, shrugging his shoulders and turning to look right at Veronica, "I just know that you're the prettiest girl I've ever seen and that moonlight makes you even prettier."

"Oh, stop," laughed Veronica, swatting him lightly on the shoulder with her right hand. "You can be so corny at times. Too many sappy movies, eh? You need to find a new scriptwriter."

They looked across the wall to the other rooftop next to Devon's. They could hear a soft, gentle cooing sound.

"Is that a pigeon coop or something over there? Billy asked, squinting his eyes trying to see through the darkness.

"Sure sounds like it," she answered. "I remember them by the thousands all flying around when I was last in Manhattan. One pooped on my brand new hat as it flew by. I swore at it but had to admire its aim."

They both laughed at that.

They each took sips from their drinks and started nibbling on the cheeses and meats on their platters.

"I'm *so* glad that you were able to come over, Billy. I've missed you and we'll be able to have a nice relaxing week. I know, my nights...and Wednesday afternoon...oh, and Saturday afternoon will be taken with the play. But I'm thinking that our relationship seems to be heading in a new direction, don't you?"

"If the direction that you're referring to is going in the same direction as my thoughts, yes, Ronnie, I agree," answered Billy. "Not sure how this long distance thing will play out, though. That has me concerned."

"I love London, Billy. I love the theater here. But, in all honesty, I do miss the States. I also love Manhattan. And Broadway, Billy...*Broadway!* We'll have time to talk about it all this week. Who knows? I just might be ready for a change."

"What about the play you're in at the moment?" asked Billy, staring up at the moon.

Veronica sighed and took a long sip from her glass.

"*Private Lives* is billed as a limited engagement. We're actually due to close at the end of November. My agent here says she has a few potential things in the works, but nothing definite yet."

The door leading downstairs opened and they could hear music and laughter coming from inside.

"Dance with me, Ronnie. Let's dance."

He took hold of her hand and drew her closer to him. He could smell her intoxicating perfume and she could smell his masculine, musky after-shave.

Someone clearing their throat behind them interrupted their long, lingering kiss.

"I hate to interrupt you two sweethearts," said Alexis, "but I'm afraid that I have to leave. My cab will be pulling up any minute now. I just wanted to say goodnight and it was so nice making your acquaintance, Billy. I shall see you again soon, I have no doubt."

She started to leave, then hesitated for a second. "Not that I'm being a big mother hen, Veronica, but remember tomorrow is matinee day, isn't it?"

Veronica let out a long sigh.

"Yes, it is. Darn, and I was having such a great time. Billy, I hate to end your first evening in London so soon, but we'll have plenty of time in the coming days. We have a whole week for fun, right? Let's make every day a surprise. Want to share our cab and drop you off at your hotel?"

Suddenly they heard a bit of commotion coming from the street below. They leaned over the wall around the roof to see two cars stopping abruptly along the street. A man from one car, followed by a man from the other slammed their cars doors shut, and ran up the front steps of a house two down from Devon's.

"I have to go," Alexis said anxiously, as she backed away from the wall. "Are you all coming with me or not?"

5

Devon Stone was awakened early in the afternoon following his party by the front doorbell ringing, followed by a loud knocking on the door. He was groggy, had more than a slight hangover and had slept on a couch in his front parlor after bidding farewell to the last of his guests. The house was a shambles. Dirty glasses and dishes everywhere and he awoke clutching a woman's shimmering black satin high-heeled shoe. He was also bare-chested. And he smiled with the memory of how he had gotten that way. The doorbell and knocking persisted.

Running his hand through his rumpled hair, he ambled to the door, opening it to reveal a pleasant-looking, dark-haired, bearded man, mid-fortyish, dressed in a dark navy suit. The man quickly held out a badge for Devon to see. He leaned in, squinted, and looked back up to the man's unsmiling face as the badge was just as quickly pulled back.

"Good afternoon, Mr. Stone," said the man in a somewhat perturbed tone. He glanced at the half-dressed Devon. "I hope I haven't disturbed you too much. I've been pounding on your door for fifteen minutes. I'm Howard Vanderhoff. Police Inspector Howard Vanderhoff. May I step inside?"

"Oh, yes, of course," responded Devon, somewhat confused. "I hope my party last night didn't cause too much commotion and aroused the ire of any neighbors. Please, do come in, Inspector." And he stepped aside allowing the man to enter.

Vanderhoff looked around and arched his eyebrows.

"Must have been quite a party. And on a Tuesday, no less," he huffed. "Let me get to the point. Do you happen to know a Mildred Winsom?"

Devon was perceptive and happened to notice a slight catch in the Inspector's voice when he mentioned the woman's name. Devon also had a sudden thought that this man looked familiar somehow. But he pushed it back in his mind. For now. And, for some reason, Devon decided to feign ignorance.

"No, Inspector, I'm not familiar with that name. Why?"

The inspector paused ever so slightly before he answered.

"She's a neighbor of yours, Mr. Stone. The station received a very strange anonymous telephone call late last night. She lives, well, lived only two houses away from yours. She was murdered, evidently last night."

"What?" Devon loudly exclaimed. "I'm flabbergasted. When? I mean, what time?"

"Our medical examiner figures it was sometime between 6 P.M. and 10. Did you happen to see or hear anything unusual around those times?"

"Are you serious, my good man?" Devon laughed. "Look around here and please, rethink that question."

"I am only doing my job, sir. I'm going from door to door along the street asking questions, just starting an investigation, as it were."

"I'm, sorry, Inspector, I didn't mean to seem impertinent. Please accept my profound apology. I can't believe it. A murder right here on our little street of years."

"Excuse me?" asked the confused inspector. "Street of years? What does *that* mean?"

Devon Stone smiled.

"I guess my writer's imagination gets a little carried away at times. Haven't you noticed the house numbers along this street? My house is 1917, the one next to mine in one direction is 1915, the next 1913. The other direction it goes 1919, 1921, and so on and so on. I noticed it before I even bought this place. The street of years. I found it funny, that's all. Nothing to it, really. So then, cause of death?"

Inspector Vanderhoff was taken aback by the sudden question. He stared at Devon for a moment.

"You know I'm not at liberty to tell you that, sir. This is an ongoing investigation."

"Oh, come on, Inspector, be a good chap. I happen to be a mystery writer. I know countless dozens of ways to kill off someone and even more ways of how to hide the bodies. Who knows? I might even be able to help you solve this heinous crime."

"We certainly don't need, nor want civilian assistance," the inspector huffed, drawing himself up to full height.

Devon put his hands on his hips and stared right back at Vanderhoof, arching one eyebrow. Vanderhoff blinked first.

"She was strangled. With a scarf. I don't remem…we don't know if it was *her* scarf or one brought by the perpetrator. We shall have to check to see if she has done any travelling."

"And what, exactly, does *that* mean, Inspector?"

"It might mean nothing, but the small tag on the scarf was in Russian. She may have purchased it locally or elsewhere. It may have been a gift. It's something to check out further. And I have said *way* too much already. Could you possibly supply me with a list of all your party guests? I suppose I should question them as well."

"Get out your notebook, Inspector. I assume that you have one. I can give you everyone's name, their addresses, their telephone numbers, and exactly what time each one arrived and departed last night. Even the ones who tried to sneak out without saying goodnight. Oh, and the wait staff I hired for the occasion."

"How do you know all that?"

"Sir, I'm very observant. Extremely, for that matter. And I have a memory that simply never fails."

Howard Vanderhoff pulled a pen and small notepad from his suit jacket. He then put on a pair of dark-rimmed reading glasses.

And that's when Devon Stone remembered where he had seen Inspector Howard Vanderhoff before.

6

Between the matinee and evening performances the day after Devon's party, Billy and Veronica scheduled to meet at the Lamb & Flag Pub where Alexis worked. The pub was a short walk from the theater. He arrived early, looking around for Alexis to order a pint of ale. He loved the aroma of old bars or, in this case, an old pub. He inhaled deeply, taking in the smell of stale smoke, beer, and old, old wood. He lit up a Lucky Strike, allowing his exhaled smoke to blend with that of centuries past.

"Has Alexis come in yet today?" he asked the barman, a grizzled man of perhaps sixty.

"No, she was supposed to be here at one and she never showed up. No call. Nothing, mate. Are you a friend, or what?" He sounded a bit miffed.

"I just met her last night at a party. She's the roommate of my girlfriend. That's okay; I'm waiting for my friend to come in any minute. Maybe she'll know why Alexis didn't show up."

The barman brought Billy a frosty mug and set it down on the bar with a loud clunk. He refilled a wooden bowl that was on the bar with salted peanuts and brought another bowl filled with something crispy-looking and placed it in front of Billy.

"What's that?" asked Billy as he leaned in closer to try to figure what the stuff was.

The barman looked at Billy like he had just come in from Mars.

"Them's pork scratchings, mate. Never seen 'em b'fore, eh?" chuckled the barman. "Try one and you'll be hooked for life, I tell ya. Just fried 'em me self, I did. Pork skin, mate, from the little piggy's hind leg, it is. Just kidding you, though. I didn't cook 'em. The dirty old cook in the back room did." And he chuckled again.

Billy took one and nibbled it slowly. Then he chewed the whole thing. Before he knew it, the bowl was empty. The old barman laughed a wheezy laugh, shaking his head.

"Told ya, I did," he said as he refilled the bowl of peanuts again.

"Interesting place here," Billy asked, just to be friendly. "I see by the sign outside that it's been here for a few hundred years."

"Yeah, right, mate. Since 1623 to be exact. Sometimes it feels as though I've been here ever since opening day. Today, for example," and he chuckled to himself. "It used to be called the Bucket of Blood. Lots of fights within these walls. Not that you're interested, but Charles Dickens was once a regular here. Him and the ghost of Marley, I presume."

•

It was 7 o'clock and his house was now returned to somewhat of an order. The servers from the night before had returned to wash and put away all the dishes, glasses and silverware. Devon had bathed, shaved and gotten himself dressed to walk over to his favorite pub a few blocks away. The doorbell ringing, the second time today, annoyed him. *Now what?* he thought. He opened the door to face a sixtyish, somewhat overweight man wearing a rumpled three-piece black suit. The jacket was open and if the man should inhale too deeply, surely the buttons on his vest would pop. There were a couple stains on the man's vest, perhaps remnants of his lunch.

"Good evening, sir," said the gentleman, "May I assume that you are a Mr. Devon Stone? And may I have a moment of your time for a few questions?"

"I am and you may. But who, sir, might *you* be?"

"Oh, so sorry, my good man," said the man, flashing a badge. "I'm Howard Vanderhoff. Police Inspector Howard Vanderhoff."

Devon stared at the person standing in front of him. He had never seen this man before in his life.

•

Billy turned around just as Veronica was coming through the front door. Two middle-aged men who seemed excited by her presence stopped her momentarily, and chatted with a lot of arm fluttering. She laughed, scribbled something on a playbill that one of them handed to her. She kissed each one politely on the cheek and headed toward Billy. He stood, shaking his head.

"Don't tell. Adoring fans, right?" he asked, leaning in to give her a firm, yet sweet kiss on the lips.

"They had just left this afternoon's performance. Obviously they were stunned to see their goddess, as they called me, out amongst you mortals. First autograph I've given all day. I see that you've started drinking without me, you lout. Where's Alexis? Did she serve you?"

"No, she's not here. The bartender seems to be more than a tad disturbed by that fact. She never called in and he's short staffed tonight."

"Really? That's not like her. By the way, just to be accurate, they aren't called bartenders here in England. They are called barmen. Anyway, I don't believe Alexis drank too much at the party last night. For that matter, I don't remember seeing her with a drink in her hand at all. We had a friendly chat in the cab after we dropped you off at your hotel, and then we went to our respective bedrooms when we got back to the flat. Now that I think about it, there wasn't a sound coming from her room this morning. She's usually an early riser and is in the bathroom before me. Not so this morning. Strange."

She glanced at the empty bowl on the bar, leaned in to sniff it.

"Don't tell me you've been eating pork scratchings! Good lord, you'll be hooked and weigh five pounds heavier by the end of the week."

•

"I assure you, Mr. Stone, I am, indeed, Police Inspector Vanderhoff. You can check with a couple of those officers two houses away to verify it," the gentleman said, producing not only a badge but also identification papers and a small note pad.

"Right, then," said a confused Devon Stone. "I haven't got a clue as to why anyone would be impersonating you, Inspector. But come on in and we will definitely try to get to the bottom of all this rigmarole," stepping aside to allow this person to enter.

"I assume, then, that this has something to do with Mildred Winsom?"

The Inspector flipped open his note pad, and looked befuddled as he glanced at it.

"Mildred *Winsom*? No, sir, it has to do with a Mildred *Wallace*."

"Little Min? Oh, good lord. What has she done now?"

"Well, sir," the Inspector said sadly, "she was murdered last night."

7

"I'll have to dash back to the theater soon," said Veronica after downing a couple Sloe Gin Fizzes. "I'll grab a quick bite at a little shop close to the theater and take it to my dressing room. They sell the best pasties I have ever tasted. But please stay here for a while and soak up some more of the atmosphere along with another Guinness. Oh, don't you *dare* leave without having their classic Toad in the Hole. It's yummy. You'll think you've died and gone to Heaven."

"Excuse me?" asked Billy with a smirk. "Toad in the Hole? Last night it was a cheese called horse poop and now this? I assume it's a dish of some kind but it sure doesn't sound very appetizing to me. Pork scratchings and now Toad in the Hole?"

Veronica laughed.

"Seriously. Try it. It's an incredible sausage dish. The sausage is cooked in a Yorkshire pudding batter. I know you like Bangers and Mash. I do, too. But trust me, you just might like this better."

She glanced at her watch and grabbed a piece of the crispy pork from the newly refilled bowl on the bar, chewing it as she left.

"I've got to run. Curtain is in sixty minutes. I hope Alexis shows up soon!"

•

Devon felt as though he had been kicked severely in the stomach. His head was spinning because of the conflicting stories from two strange men, one of whom was an imposter.

"I don't understand, Inspector. What in blazes is going on? First I'm told that one of my neighbors who I do *not* know, Mildred Winsom, was murdered last night. Is that true or not?"

"I certainly don't know anything about this Winsom lady to which you are referring. I shall be going down from house to house seeking information. That's all I can say at this point. Frankly, I'm as confused as you are regarding this other conundrum. A man claiming to be me? Why? But, I can assure you, sir, that your neighbor Mildred Wallace was, indeed murdered last night. Another neighbor notice a smashed in window at the rear of Mrs. Wallace's house and alerted the police. When they arrived they found her front door ajar. Cautiously the police entered and found her on the floor in the center hallway. I was then alerted and, well, here I am."

"I know I probably shouldn't ask this or even expect an honest reply, but what was the cause of death?" asked Devon, at this point close to tears.

"You're right, I probably should not reveal too much information at this point but, Mr. Stone, I know who you are. Well, my wife does anyway. She has read and loved all your books. Frankly, I shy away from murder mysteries, as it were, well, because of my day job. Oh, in answer to your question, Mrs. Wallace was strangled. When did you last see the victim, if I may ask?"

"I had a party here last night for many of my friends. She was here. She left my house at 12:18."

The inspector wrote something in his notepad.

"So she left here at approximately 12:15 last night..."

"Not approximately. It was precisely at 12:18."

The inspector looked puzzled.

"And how do you know it was precisely that time?"

"Let's just say that I'm very observant and have a...well, a very good memory. And let's just leave it at that, shall we?"

The inspector stared at Devon for a few moments.

"Hmmm, so then, a party was in progress. Obviously no one was going to hear anything going on two doors away later that evening, like breaking glass."

"Obviously."

Devon stared back at the inspector for a few moments.

"I shall check into that other neighbor, Mr. Stone, and if anything else seems untoward I shall return to ask some further questions if I may."

"By all means, Inspector. By all means. Little Min...I'm sorry, Mrs. Wallace was a dear friend of mine."

Mildred Wallace was more than a dear friend to Devon but considering the very unusual situation, he would say no more.

"One question, Inspector, if you can answer it before you go. You said that my friend was strangled. Was it with a scarf, by any chance?"

"No, definitely by some very strong hands, judging by the bruising. Why do you ask?"

"Just curious, Inspector. That's all. Curious."

He ushered the inspector out with the promise from him that more information would be forthcoming, perhaps sooner than the newspapers would blare it out to the world. Devon was devastated and even closer to tears than he was a few moments earlier when a thought suddenly struck him. It was a question that had gone *unasked* by the inspector. Inspector #1 earlier this afternoon, when told of the party, requested a complete list of the guests. Inspector #2 did not. Why? The mystery writer in him answered his own question. Inspector #1 was seeking someone out. Someone who, more than likely, had been at the party.

Devon knew exactly who that person was. But *that* name wasn't on his list.

8

By sheer happenstance, Clovis James was entering the Lamb & Flag at the precise moment that Veronica was leaving, licking her fingers. She, of course, did not know who he was but he certainly knew who *she* was. He smiled and nodded to her as they passed each other and she, in turn, smiled politely back. *A fan being discrete,* she thought to herself as she walked back to the theater.

Billy was, indeed, enjoying the Toad in a Hole and would have surely licked the platter if he could. He asked for a third pint of ale and sat back to enjoy the atmosphere of the now quickly filling and noisy pub, lighting up another cigarette as he did so. He forced himself to resist the bowls of peanuts and, especially, the bits of fried pork skins.

Clovis looked around and appeared to be either confused or disappointed. He approached the barman.

"Charlie, where's Alexis? I thought she'd be here by now."

"She never showed up, Mr. James. No bloody phone call or anything either. Not like her at all, all I can say."

Billy couldn't help but overhear this short conversation.

"Excuse me, sir, are you a friend of Alexis Morgan?" asked Billy. "I'm not trying to be rude or anything and don't take this the wrong way if you are her boyfriend, but I was looking for her also."

Clovis James gave Billy a cold stare and then furrowed his brows.

"And who, sir, are *you?*" asked the critic.

Billy stood up and extended his hand.

"I'm Billy Bennett, sir, and Alexis is the roommate of my girlfriend, Veronica Barron."

Clovis's eyebrows immediately shot up. He exchanged a quick glance with the barman as they both turned to look at Billy.

"Be careful, young man. Be very careful," said Clovis James sternly as he turned and abruptly left the building.

•

Billy met with Veronica following the evening performance and took a taxi back to her flat.

"How well do you know Alexis?" asked Billy, as they rode, a bit concerned after his brief encounter with that man at the pub.

"Well, we've exchanged stories about our time here in England and chatted about our jobs but, frankly, she hasn't been all that forthcoming. I guess I've done most of the talking. I'm good at that, as you know. Why do you ask that now?"

Billy related his brief chat with a man called Mr. James. He tried to describe him but it drew a blank as far as Ronnie was concerned. She just shrugged her shoulders.

"I don't know. She has never mentioned having a boyfriend or anything like that. She works long and late hours. She was very excited when we first started chatting at the pub about my profession. Actually, she hadn't heard of *me*, but she said she was a big fan of Gregory Montgomery and had been following his career. She had been staying in a small, cramped flat, and she complained about its nastiness. So I offered her a second bedroom in *my* flat. Not that I really needed it, but she was thrilled to be able to share the rent with me and tell everyone she knew an American actress. I thought it would be fun."

"Interesting," said Billy. "I suppose."

The cab pulled up to the flat and Billy paid the driver.

They were hoping to find Alexis there, safe and sound, but that wasn't to be. Veronica knocked on her bedroom door, at first softly, then louder.

"I hate to violate her privacy but maybe she's ill or worse behind this door," Veronica said with concern as she turned toward Billy.

She tried the door handle and it was unlocked. She slowly opened the door and reached for the light switch. The bed was disheveled, the closet door open, but no Alexis. Billy followed her into the room, looking around.

"Ronnie, what do you suppose this means, have any idea?" he said as he picked up a small scrap of paper that had been on the nightstand. She took the paper and read it.

M.W. 1913 – definitely

Veronica shook her head.

"I haven't a clue, but that's not Alexis's handwriting. That I *do* know. What is it? Someone's initials and a birthdate, perhaps?"

Billy quickly did the math in his head.

"Well, *if* it's a birthdate, whoever M.W. is would be 39. But we're just making wild guesses about that, aren't we?"

"Just put it back where you found it, Billy. This is none of our business. I feel very guilty poking around in her room. It's not nice. I'm sure she'll show up at any time. It's probably nothing to be concerned about."

When, after two days, there had been no sign of Alexis they grew concerned.

9

Mildred Winsom checked into a small inn midway between London and Stonehenge under an assumed name. The inn was neither her first choice nor the second but, with tourist season still winding down, vacancies were scarce. She went into the red telephone booth that stood to the far end of the inn's car park and placed a call to her married lover, Jacob Everett. And then she waited.

Two hours later a knock on her door awakened Mildred from her slumber.

"Sorry, Millie, I got here as quickly as I could. You know, having to make the usual excuses. You understand."

Jacob Everett was 45, tall, dark-haired and bearded.

After a quick peck on the cheek, he followed her back into her room, closing the door behind him.

"Look at this," Mildred said to him, handing him a piece of paper.

He removed dark-rimmed reading glasses from his jacket pocket and read what was presented to him. A blurry black and white photograph and a scribbled name.

"You see?" Mildred asked. "She's one of them. She's a witch, for sure."

"But she's awfully young, don't you think? I mean that was almost ten years ago."

"Some of us age better than others. I agree, but I recognize the name. At least the last name, anyway. I thought she was dead. We were *told* she was dead. It's *got* to be her. After her rude visit a few nights ago, I was convinced that she knows. At least in part. As I told you later that evening, she tried to pretend that she had gotten the wrong address, but I didn't fall for that nonsense. I tried to detain her but she got away too quickly. I showed you that scarf that I had grabbed from around her neck as she tried to run. After you and Gregory arrived later that night, and I relayed the incident, I knew we had to go into hiding quickly. She's got to be dealt with. She's got to disappear. Permanently. Just like all the others."

"I got the list of all those people at the party. Her name isn't on it," answered Jacob Everett, shaking his head.

"Well, of course not. I didn't think that it would be. No doubt she's using an alias. She is very smart. Very shrewd. I am convinced that Aleksandra Markarova *was* at that party. And furthermore, I am *really* convinced that a few more of her conspirators were there as well. One of them has already been dealt with. And what ruse did you use to get that list?"

"Oh, I played the role very well, indeed. I really kicked it up a notch, I must say. I got a toy badge from one of my tykes, flashed it quickly, and told Stone that I was Police Inspector Howard Vanderhoff."

"You're an idiot!"

•

"It was at the Holly Bush pub where I saw that man pretending to be you, Inspector," Devon said to Inspector #2. He had telephoned *this* Inspector at the police station.

"I was having drinks with my publisher when I glanced around to observe a table where some loud laughter was distracting. That man, the *first* Inspector Vanderhoff, was getting somewhat amorous with a woman sitting next to him. I smiled at his flirtatiousness although I thought he should have been a bit more discrete about it. This particular pub is more like a private home, less raucous than some, and I thought he should show a bit more decorum. It was Monday, 16th of June, at 9:22 when I first noticed him."

"I'm not even going to ask how you can be so precise, Mr. Stone, I'll take your word for it."

"The woman appeared to be younger than the gentleman in question. I, personally, didn't find her that particularly attractive. She had black,

black hair, possibly dyed I thought, and a slightly crooked nose. She was wearing a fancy frock and he was wearing a dark suit. Now that I remember it, it was the same suit he was wearing when he came to my door a few days ago. He had just put on a pair of dark-rimmed reading glasses to peruse the menu."

Although Devon could not see it, the inspector was shaking his head. *What's with this man's memory?* Vanderhoff was thinking to himself.

"They were joined shortly after that by an older, heavyset woman. The couple appeared to calm down at that point and acted a bit more refined. Oh, not that this can help in any way, but the bearded man had called his paramour Millie."

•

"I had just seen the Inspector's name in the morning's paper, Millie, and I thought it would be fun. And a bit of a tease, as it were. When I mentioned the scarf I had expected a reaction of some sort. There wasn't any."

"Really? They're a bunch of crafty actors, aren't they? Shrewd to the core."

Mildred Winsom stopped pacing and stood silent for a moment, pondering what Jacob had just told her.

"Sometimes, Jacob, I simply do *not* understand the things you do. Or *not* do. I have a logical question regarding your illogical behavior. You were right there, alone in his house with him. No one else was around. Why the hell didn't you just kill him then and there and be done with it?"

"I just wanted to toy with them all a bit longer. Besides, I thought that you'd like to have the honor of doing him in. In your own personal style. Won't that be fun, Millie?"

"And what would have happened if Devon Stone actually knew the *real* Inspector? Did you even stop to think about that?"

"Well then, I probably would have shot him between the eyes and made a hasty retreat."

"I repeat. You're an idiot. But I suppose I care for you, idiot that you are. Anyway, I've packed up my things and shall be staying here for the time being. Being that you mentioned my quote-unquote *murder* to Stone, he'll no doubt pass that information along to the *real* Inspector Vanderhoff. I imagine there will be a lot of fuss about that fairly quickly. Especially since I have now vacated the place. That will surely open up a whole *new* can of worms. I hate to resort to clichés, but we'll cross that rickety old bridge when we get to it."

"I mentioned your name to see if there was any reaction from Stone," Jacob Everett explained. "I thought that if they had you pegged there would be some sort of a response, you know, like a sly smile, an arched eyebrow or something. I watched his face. But there was none. No reaction whatsoever. Perhaps they haven't been able to zero in on you yet. Perhaps they won't."

"Then perhaps I'm lucky for the time being," Mildred said, "or perhaps Stone is a cool-as-a-cucumber actor, putting one over on *you*. You remember it took us quite a while to find out about *him*. What a shock to discover that he lived only two houses away from me! Of course, I knew that Devon Stone the famous author lived close by, but never thought that he was...well, now we know what else he is."

She stopped pacing back and forth and stood in front of Jacob, unbuttoning her blouse.

"No matter what, we need to stay sharp. Stay on our toes. Do you need to rush back to dear old wifey tonight or can you stay a bit longer?"

"No, I'm, quote-unquote, at an out-of-town conference for a few days. She's so naïve and believes everything I tell her."

"She's an idiot."

⋅

"That's intriguing that you said the man, this imposter as it were, called the woman with him at the pub Millie," mused Inspector Vanderhoff. "This other woman who was supposedly murdered two house from yours was Mildred something or other, right?

"Yes, a Mildred Winsom. I have never met that woman, nor seen her. I have no idea who she is. Unless, of course, *she* was that Millie with Inspector #1."

"Hmmmm," they both said that at the same time.

10

The irony of the situation is that Mildred Winsom had, at one time, been an exceedingly sweet woman. Her two passions were gardening and cooking. With the help of her first husband's money, she opened a small florist shop in Covent Garden, *Millie's Florets*. With the close proximity of the Royal Opera House, several other theaters and shops, it became quite a success within a very short time. Her husband, Oliver Weston, hated the name of the shop but convinced her to make an addition to it. He absolutely loved the pasties that she had been making at home since they were married, and was certain that others would agree. They were more delicious than any others he had eaten elsewhere, including the ones sold in various shops around Covent Garden. He convinced her on the idea of setting up a portion of her shop to sell them as well as the flowers. Mildred thought the combination was an odd one, but she said that she would try it out for a few weeks to see if it might work.

It worked beautifully. She could hardly keep up with making the pasties and selling out by noontime every day. She hired an assistant for the floral part of her business, while she baked the pasties at home, bringing them to the shop early in the morning and then another batch later in the afternoon.

She soon discovered, totally by accident, that Oliver had another idea. And that idea involved her assistant, Ida Leiberman.

A nasty scene ensued between the three of them, ending when Mildred threatened to use her favorite butcher knife on both Ida's neck and a very private part of Oliver's anatomy.

So, divorce number one, done.

With Ida and Oliver now out of the picture, shortly thereafter she met and fell in love with a bookstore owner two doors down from her still-flourishing florist/pasty shop. A quick courtship lead to a quick marriage. Millie was happy once again. She joked that with her now two marriages and her maiden name of Winsom, she never had to change the monograms on her towels. Aaron Wasserstrom adored her flowers and her cooking. And after a year of wedded bliss Mildred discovered that Aaron now also adored *his* assistant…Allen Spiegelberg. Adored him a little *too* much.

Divorce number two, done.

A true Protestant, through and through, she was torn. Was it both her faith in God and good deeds that would assure her being welcomed into Heaven? Or was it simply her faith alone and to Hell with good deeds?

And, to add insult to injury, husband number one still legally owned *Millie's Florets*. He sold the shop out from under Mildred's nose. To Ida Leiberman.

Betrayal and distrust bloomed as vividly as any of her flowers.

She sued and actually was rewarded with a sizeable settlement before the case went to trial. She had also received a substantial sum from husband number two if she would keep his nasty illicit situation private. With the settlements along with wise investments, Mildred Winsom was able to open and successfully run a little shop in Covent Garden selling only her sought-after pasties. Her little meat pies were favored among theater patrons heading into the Drury Lane.

Aware that she had missed several clues along the way throughout both marriages, Mildred picked up a trend to her unhappiness and let it fester. She had been lied to, cheated on, embarrassed and, basically, disgraced.

She fell asleep every night with the hatred growing inside her mind. She awoke every morning with it even stronger. And more destructive.

Although she was politically naïve and hadn't fully understood the consequences and horrendous outcome of the Holocaust, she had secretly embraced Hitler's Final Solution.

Mildred Winsom became a truly vindictive person.

11

Jacob Everett met Mildred Winsom while she still owned her florist shop, before all the nasty divorce business began with husband number one. He intended to buy a nice floral arrangement for his wife's birthday but he was smitten as soon as he began speaking with Millie. She was sweet, friendly, and strangely alluring. Attributes his wife no longer possessed.

Jacob continued being a customer, first with the flowers and then, especially, for the pasties. His heart grew fonder as his appetite grew larger. When the situation became nasty with Millie's husband number two, Jacob was a good listener and became a friendly, welcome shoulder on which to cry.

As a child, Jacob Everett had been too good of a listener, however. His father, Alexander, was the epitome of the term bigot. Every ethnicity on the planet would be recipients of hateful verbal diatribes almost on a daily basis. At dinner table conversations, every night, Alexander Everett would spout out the most hateful things about one group or another, whether it was racial, political or religion-wise. Jews were just a notch above Negroes. Jacob believed every word. By the time he was a teenager, Jacob had heard practically every ethnic slur in the English language. He idolized his father and turned into just as much of a bigoted person if not more so.

After Millie's divorce number two, Jacob commiserated wholeheartedly and a new, deadly, hateful bond was formed.

12

Sunday, and Veronica didn't have any shows to do today. The theater was dark on Sundays. She planned on sleeping late, meeting Billy for lunch and touring London like a tourist. She grumbled to herself when the phone started ringing at 8 A.M.

"Veronica, I am so very sorry to disturb you like this," said Alexis. "I know you must have many questions."

Veronica first responded with a gasp.

"Yes, I *have*, Alexis. For one, where in blazes are you and why have you disappeared so suddenly? I have worried myself sick over you! Thank God that you're alive."

"Again, I apologize. I certainly never intended to drag you into this subterfuge but now you are the only one I can turn to. The only one, I feel, who is not being followed."

"What did you just say? What do you mean? Followed? By whom?"

"I need your help. If you are willing, that is."

"Are you in any trouble, Alexis?" asked Veronica nervously.

"Trouble, no. Danger, yes. I will explain if we can get together today."

"Well, yes," answered Veronica, trepidation in her voice. "When and where?"

"Can you and Billy hire a car for the day?" asked Alexis.

"Of course. I think there is a car-hire location a couple blocks from our flat. But where have you been all this time?"

"I've been staying at a friend's cottage in Amesbury, but that's not important at the moment. I just can't come back into London just yet. That's why I need your assistance."

"Okay," responded Veronica, again cautiously. "I repeat, when and where?"

"Come out to Stonehenge. I will meet you there. I'll try to get there shortly and wait for a few hours. If you don't show up by three, I'll leave. Then, unfortunately, I may have to seek another avenue for help."

•

Mildred Winsom and Jacob Everett had slept in later than they intended but they were in no particular hurry to do anything. Jacob knew of a little café a couple miles from the inn in which they were staying and they were both hungry. With Jacob driving, they were just about to pull out onto A303 when Mildred suddenly shrieked.

"Look!" she called out loudly, pointing to a car that had just passed heading in the direction of Wiltshire. "Isn't that her? I swear that's Aleksandra Markarova in that car. I can't believe it. I am dead certain that's her. Follow her, but at a distance. I don't want her to know she's being followed. This might be our lucky day!"

•

"Why do these fools drive on the wrong side of the road over here?" laughed Billy as he maneuvered their rental car through the streets of London.

Soon, they were out of the city and heading westward as the sun overhead slowly turned to clouds and then to a drizzly rain. The rain turned into downpours for a few miles and then, by the time they reached the muddy car park for Stonehenge, the sun had returned. A mobile tea-bar was set up in the car park, and a few tourists were enjoying a cup after roaming through the mysterious circle of stones. A contentious and long-sought excavation and restoration plan was about to begin, as was evident by large pieces of equipment lying about. While the project itself had yet to begin, visitors to the site had to contend with stepping over and around bits of scaffolding and digging apparatuses. Billy and Veronica started walking amongst the huge stones being mindful of where they stepped. The tourist season was definitely coming to a close as they were amongst only about a dozen other people viewing the massive stones. They stopped wandering from time to time to look up at one piece or another towering over them.

"This place is fascinating, isn't it?" asked Billy, looking in all directions. "Let's spend more time exploring after we meet up with Alexis. I've read about this place for years and I can't believe we're actually here. Too bad we don't have a camera."

They approached the far side of the gigantic circle when Alexis stepped suddenly from behind one of tall stones, startling them both. Veronica rushed to hug her and started admonishing her for her disappearance.

"Again, I am so sorry about this whole situation," said Alexis. Only this time when she spoke it wasn't with a carefully enunciated English accent. "Forgive me, please, for involving you."

"Wait," said Billy, standing back and looking at Alexis. "What is that accent?"

"Please, I shall explain when I can. But will you please, please get this package to Devon Stone?"

She handed Veronica a small thin box wrapped in brown paper. Hesitantly, Veronica accepted it.

"Why can't you give it to him yourself? Or why can't you just mail it to him?" asked Billy.

"Too many questions for now," answered Alexis. "Too many answers still to be determined. Actually, the less you know, the safer you will be. Trust me. Just, please, Devon will know what to do with it."

"But. But that accent, Alexis," Billy began. "What is it and who *are* you?"

"I am…" she began to answer just as a shot was fired from behind them and a bullet struck the stone mere inches from Alexis's head.

Veronica let out a frightened little squeal as they all ducked behind the stone and parts of scaffolding as more bullets were fired. Chunks of stone splintered and fell around them and Billy protected Veronica with his own body. The other tourists scattered in fear.

"Well, damn! I'm used to getting fired at on the battlefield but certainly not in the middle of a tourist attraction! Stay down and stay back both of you!"

The firing stopped momentarily, Billy assuming that the gunman was perhaps reloading. He slowly peered around from their hiding place and saw a tall bearded man inching his way toward them, dodging in and out of the massive stones. The man was one large, tall stone away from them when Billy heard and felt movement directly behind him, almost at his back. He turned to look just at the exact moment that Alexis fired a revolver toward the approaching shooter. With the gunshot still ringing in his ear, Billy's head whipped back around in time to see the gaping hole in the middle of the man's forehead before he plopped over backwards. By the time he swung around once again, Alexis…or whoever she might be was gone.

By the time the police arrived a mere five minutes later, Mildred Winsom had also vanished and Jacob Everett lay dead on the ground.

•

Sometimes it's not the things that one says to the police that are important, but the things that one does *not* say.

Billy had instantly recognized the revolver that Alexis used. It was a Nagant M1895. Russian. But he decided to feign ignorance, at least for the time being and until they might be able to figure out what was going on. Who *was* Alexis? And why is she being targeted? And by whom? He and Veronica were the last of the tourists to be interrogated by the police officer in charge.

"So you do not know the person who killed this man?" asked a husky police officer.
"No, sir," answered Veronica, succinctly.

That wasn't a lie, because who *is* this Alexis, or whoever she might? At this point neither Billy nor Veronica had a clue.

"We do not, officer," Billy said in turn, trying to sound a bit rattled. "We were simply strolling through this amazing place when all of a sudden shots rang out. Having been through a war, sir, I took immediate action and we hit the deck! I mean I pushed my girlfriend, here, down on the ground for cover and safety. And the ground was slippery, too, from the recent rain shower."

The police officer had seen that Veronica's dress and Billy's pants were splattered with mud.

"We kept our heads down and just hoped that whoever was shooting was not going on some crazed rampage shooting everyone in sight. It was frightening, to say the least, sir."

"Yes, right. Indeed. I completely understand, young man. Horrible experience, I'm sure. So sorry that you visitors had to endure this horrible incident. Don't let it tarnish your thoughts about our beautiful country. These things are not frequent occurrences, I assure you. Now then, I know from speaking with the others here that all of the cars in the car park are accounted for, yours included. Which leaves a major question."

"How did the shooter get here?" asked Veronica.

"Exactly right, young lady. Exactly right. I can't believe that he simply walked here from god-knows-where. His car is gone. Meaning, of course, he did not arrive here alone. His companion, or companions, whoever that might be, has fled."

13

Veronica had hidden the small package that Alexis had given to them in her pocketbook. Once they were back in the car, heading toward London again, she took out the package and examined it. Written on the brown wrapping were an address, 1917 Carlingford Road, and a telephone number. They both made the assumption that these were Devon Stone's. She carefully shook it, producing a muffled rattle. They both made a decision.

•

A day or so following his last conversation with Inspector Vanderhoff, Devon Stone had made a decision after receiving a cryptic telegram. Things were beginning to heat up and a possible conclusion to the situation was fast approaching. He packed enough clothes for five days and called his next-door neighbor.

•

Upon arriving back in the city, Billy checked out of his hotel room, returned the rental car, and moved his luggage into Veronica's apartment.

"At this point, we can assume that nobody knows about our involvement, such as it is," said Veronica, "at least I'm *hoping* we can assume that."

"And I'll feel much safer protecting you, if I can, from whatever or whoever," Billy answered almost matter-of-factly. "You'll be back on stage every night next week and then get back here and lock up everything that's lockable as soon as you get in. I've got to fly back home to make some further arrangements but I'll be on the very next flight back here as soon as possible. Don't call Devon Stone until I return. I'm sure a day or two can't hurt. I hope."

He sent a telegram and headed to London Airport.

•

Having fled Stonehenge practically before the gun smoke had settled, Alexis drove as quickly as she could to her friend's cottage taking a circuitous route to make sure she wasn't being followed. She pulled her car into the short driveway and entered the front door just as her friend was entering from the rear, carrying a basket of freshly picked tomatoes, probably the last of the season because of their lackluster appearance.

"Well?" he asked.

"I gave them the package but not without incident, unfortunately," she answered breathlessly.

The man set the basket on the kitchen table.

"Really? Details, please," said Clovis James.

•

After eighteen hours and ten minutes, with stops in Shannon and Gander, Billy rushed off his Pan Am Stratocruiser flight and ran, as quickly as he could, passing through customs and the crowded Idlewild Airport to baggage claim. His friend was waiting for him and they spotted each other immediately.

"Thanks *so* much for coming way out here to get me," Billy said, shaking his friend's hand vigorously and firmly.

"I didn't think twice about it, buddy, after getting your telegram," answered Peyton Chase, a fellow pilot and ex-army companion. "Couldn't tell much from your short words, but what's up?"

"Let me grab my suitcase and I'll fill you in on the drive back home."

Peyton Chase was the same age as Billy, a bit shorter, a bit heavier, and much more muscular. They had been boyhood friends, growing up just a few doors apart in Dover, New Jersey. Having enlisted together, gone through the war together, they now shared a small two-bedroom bachelor apartment not too far from their respective childhood homes. Of the two, women often thought Peyton the more handsome, with his rippling muscles, dark brown hair and smoldering dark brown eyes. No doubt, he was a charmer. He had lost his virginity while still in high school, but was gentleman enough not to brag. Not *too* much, anyway. As dapper as Billy was, Peyton was more of the rough-around-the-edges type, favoring dungarees, flannel shirts in the winter and T-shirts in the summer, and his well-worn old bomber jacket.

Together, they had opened a small gun shop shortly after returning from the war. Just off the main street of town, it was a few doors down from a very popular Italian restaurant and did a fair amount of drop-in business. While their inventory dealt mostly with hunting rifles, they carried a small amount of pistols and revolvers. Their knowledge of weaponry was encyclopedic.

"I've got to hit the bank first thing in the morning," said Billy, running up the front porch steps to their apartment building. "I need enough money to tide me over for a while and then I need to hightail it right back to London."

"Do you need any help over there?" asked Peyton. "I'll do anything you need me for."

"No, pal, not yet anyway. We don't even *know* what the hell is going on. I hate to leave you in the lurch, manning the store alone. I'll make it up to you, I promise. I feel guilty about the time I've taken off already."

"Don't worry about it, buddy," smiled Peyton, "That situation has me scratching my head, too. Do what you have to do and come back safe and sound. We made it through a damn war, what's a little intrigue? Fun, perhaps. Who knows, eh?"

"Can that jalopy of yours make another trip out to Idlewild tomorrow?" Billy laughed.

"Hey, watch it, friend!" Peyton smirked. "That good old Chevy has seen a lotta action. Front seat and back. It can take another hump or two, on the road or otherwise."

They both laughed and decided to go down to that Italian restaurant for dinner.

•

When Veronica got to the theater Monday evening she discovered that her leading man, Gregory Montgomery, had called complaining of laryngitis. His understudy, Christopher Blaze, would be performing at tonight's performance. Veronica didn't think anything of it and started applying her makeup and doing her voice exercises.

Christopher Blaze was as well liked by the London audiences as Gregory Montgomery. They were both extremely handsome and equally as talented. Both had dark, wavy hair and deep, booming voices. And they were both equally infatuated with themselves. For that matter, a certain theater critic was determined to discover if Gregory and Christopher were, indeed, actually infatuated with each other. The two of them were often seen together out and about doing the late night party scene. Sometimes they appeared to be *very* close to each other.

While Montgomery was strictly a classically trained stage actor, Christopher Blaze, ne Clarence Birdwhistle, had appeared on-screen in two frivolous little comedies starring Alec Guinness.

As it turned out, Christopher Blaze covered for Gregory Montgomery at Tuesday's performance, Wednesday matinee and also the Wednesday evening performance. Veronica began to think about Gregory's absence. It wasn't like him to miss out on all that applause from sold-out houses.

•

After eighteen hours and thirty-five minutes, with stops in Gander and Shannon, a very groggy Billy Bennett slowly walked down the steps from his Pan Am flight to face the chilly, drizzly London air. Another stamp in his passport and he headed out to the taxi stand. The cab ride from the airport to Veronica's apartment was slow and annoying. The traffic was especially bad and Billy's temper seemed to match it.

He knew Veronica would be on stage by the time he got to the apartment, but she had given him a key. He entered and went to the bedroom that had been Alexis's. It had been straightened up and most of Alexis's things had been shoved, but neatly, into the closet. He unpacked his suitcase, tucking the two pistols, a Browning Hi-Power and a Beretta, beneath his underwear in one of the drawers. He and Peyton had debated which gun he should bring with him. Peyton favored the Hi-Power, with its 13-round magazine capacity, and Billy favored the newly released Beretta 950, a semi-automatic pistol. So he had packed them both. He brought ammunition for both as well. And a lot of it, just in case. His eyes were getting heavier by the minute. After unpacking, he simply fell back onto the bed and was asleep almost immediately.

An hour later Veronica gently shaking him awakened him and interrupted a dream about Stonehenge.

"What are you doing in *this* bedroom, cowboy?" she laughed.

He slowly opened his eyes and looked around, at first not knowing where he was.

"Oh. What? Oh, uh...I didn't want to be too presumptuous, Ronnie."

"Oh, for goodness sake, Billy. This is not Victorian England you know. This is 1952. We're grown adults. And besides, I've already seen you naked."

A silly little grin slowly crept across his face.

•

Billy's thoughts quickly flashed back to early June. He had met Veronica in Paris for a long weekend. She hadn't begun the run of *Private Lives* yet and she had invited him to come over for a romantic getaway if he could. He could. And he did.

It would be an expensive trip, but Billy felt that it was worth it. His best friend and business partner, Peyton Chase, had just returned from *his* romantic getaway weekend in the Poconos, although it hadn't played out the way he had anticipated. Peyton's fiancé used the trip to soften the blow. She was breaking off the engagement. He and Billy had gotten roaring drunk together upon his return and now Peyton needed to get his mind off things. Taking care of the gun shop in Billy's absence would be ideal.

Veronica booked them into the small, venerable old Hotel Brighton on the rue de Rivoli. Their tiny wrought iron balcony on their 5th floor room overlooked the Tuileries Gardens. From the balcony, looking to the left a few blocks down and they saw the Louvre. Looking to the right and slightly at an angle, a mile or so away stood the Eiffel Tower. If they leaned *way* out and looked further to the right they could barely see the top of the Arc de Triomphe. She couldn't have picked a more romantic spot. Their bedroom had a huge brass bed that squeaked loudly with even the slightest movement and their small private bathroom had a clawfoot tub that could just barely fit two.

Walking arm in arm throughout the magnificent city, up the Champs-Élysées, down the narrow side streets, they would often see buildings still pockmarked with bullet holes and missing chips of concrete from various skirmishes during the war. Repairs were still underway. As they strolled they hit upon, totally by accident, a little sidewalk café-restaurant that intrigued them by the name alone. *Au Chien Qui Fume*. The Smoking Dog. So named by the owner in 1920 that owned two dogs, a cigar-smoking poodle and a pipe-smoking terrier. Or so the story went. They dined there three times during their stay. After each meal, as they sipped the best coffee, Billy sat back in his seat, enjoying a cigarette. Veronica laughingly called him her smoking dog.

Waking up on their last morning before they returned to their respective countries, Billy got out of bed, stretched, yawned, lit up a Lucky Strike and padded, naked, out onto their little balcony, leaning his elbows on the railing as he smoked.

"You *do* realize, don't you," called Veronica, still in bed, "that the balcony railing is an open-rung? I think you have the cutest butt that I've ever seen, however I'm not so sure how the Frenchmen on the street below might feel about your other parts."

Billy retreated.

They decided to visit the Eiffel Tower once more before checking out and heading to the airport. As they meandered along they talked about the next time Billy would come back overseas, this time to London.

"I'll be back sometime in September. I'll stay a week. I want to catch your play and revisit some sights I haven't seen since the war. I'll check into a hotel, though. I know we've been…well, extremely friendly, so to speak, but I won't feel terribly comfortable with your roommate there at your place. I think that it would be awkward."

"Oh, please, Billy, that's so Victorian. I'm sure she wouldn't think anything of it."

"Maybe after I meet her and she and I get a bit more acquainted. I know, it sounds goofy coming from a guy, doesn't it? But that's what I'll do. We'll take it a step at a time, okay?"

"If it will make you feel better, who am I to disagree? I'll bet that one way or the other, you'll end up staying at my place," and she laughed.

As they approached the Eiffel Tower they could see a lot of commotion around the base. A crowd of people, police cars and an ambulance. Obviously the Tower was closed off for some reason. Not knowing if the man closest to them spoke English or not, Billy asked what was going on. What had just happened? Trying to make himself understood, he shrugged his shoulders and pointed at the vehicles with their emergency light ablaze.

The man obviously *didn't* speak English, but he understood what Billy was asking. He gestured wildly pointing back and forth to the top of the Tower and then to the ground. He was wildly trying to explain what had happened but, although it was totally in French, one word came through clearly. It may have been pronounced differently, but it really needed no translation: *suicide.*

•

The jolt of that last, tragic moment in his memory brought Billy back to the present.

14

Early the next morning they called Devon Stone's number. They let it ring twenty times before they hung up.

"Maybe it's too early and he had a late night," Veronica said, looking at Billy and shrugging her shoulders.

Billy lit up a Lucky Strike and offered one to Veronica. She shook her head. Waiting fifteen minutes, she tried Stone's number once again. No answer. They waited another hour, with a little amorous playing and brewing a pot of coffee during that time, and dialed the number again. And, again, no answer.

"Well, then," said Billy with his hands planted firmly on his hips, "I say we get a cab and go over to his place. Alexis, or whoever she is, surely would want Stone to hear about that incident at Stonehenge."

"It was in the newspapers, Billy. You were going back and forth between here and the States when it hit the front page. The British press loves good, juicy murders. I think that if Jack the Ripper were alive today he'd be paid royally for the film rights to his life story. The victim's name was in the paper. Everson or Everett, or something like that. I think his first name was Jacob if I can remember correctly. He was married and had a couple of kids. I can't even imagine why he was trying to kill Alexis, though. His wife claimed that he was out of town on business. Supposedly he worked as a travel agent. Fortunately, *our* names were *not* mentioned anywhere in the press. I was astounded, and pleased, by that. I guess the officer who interrogated us there failed to pass our names along. Devon Stone, however, has no idea about our involvement there."

They tried calling the number one more time. No answer.

•

They asked the cabbie to please wait. They were simply going to give Devon Stone the package and make a hasty retreat. That was their plan, anyway. They climbed the twelve steps to his front door and rang the bell. They waited. They rang it again. And waited. They looked at each other and Billy shrugged his shoulders.

The cabbie honked the horn of his car. Billy turned and held up one finger, as in *please wait, just one minute.*

They rang the bell again, and then started knocking on the door. No answer. Billy started pounding on the door, harder.

The front door to the next house opened suddenly.

"You can stop that damnable pounding, young man," shouted a cantankerous old man with rumpled grey hair. "He's not home. He's on holiday. Been gone all week. He asked me to water his plants while he's gone."

"Do you know where he went?" asked Veronica.

"I do not," answered the man.

"Do you know how to reach him?" asked Billy.

"I do not," answered the man.

"Do you know when he'll return?" asked Veronica.

"I do not," answered the neighbor.

"What *do* you know?" asked Billy almost facetiously.

"I know that you're annoying the bloody hell out of me, now please go away!" said the man as he slammed his door shut.

"That's just so bizarre," said Veronica. "Why would Mr. Stone suddenly go on vacation if he knew something very intriguing was going on. You know that one of his neighbors was murdered the night of that party we attended. And Alexis was involved somehow, I feel certain now."

She stood there thinking for a second. The cabbie honked once again. Billy, again, motioned to him with a finger. A different finger this time.

"You know, something that neighbor just said has me shaking my head," said Veronica with a small frown appearing on her forehead. "He said that Mr. Stone asked him to water his plants. I realize the house was jam-packed with people the night of that party but, for the life of me, I don't recall seeing a single plant anywhere in that house. Not a one."

They started walking down the steps toward the cab.

"Well," said Billy, "perhaps it was all those plants on that huge rooftop. That place was like a botanical garden up there."

"Billy, think about it. This is London. It rains practically every hour on the hour here. You don't need to water a rooftop garden, for Pete's sake!"

•

Mildred Winsom was beyond distraught. For two reasons. She had witnessed the murder of her secret lover. And his killer had escaped. Vanished before Mildred could see where she went. She, herself, had managed a hasty getaway before anyone noticed her. Apparently no one had mentioned to the police that a witness had departed the scene. Although she had recognized the woman who shot Jacob, she couldn't see who it was that the woman was with at the time. Too much confusion after the shooting started. Since the Stonehenge incident, she had moved to two different small, off the beaten path inns, using different assumed names each time.

•

Veronica unlocked the door to her apartment, still with questions rattling around in her brain. Billy followed her in, lighting up another cigarette as he did so. Veronica took that small package intended for Devon Stone from her pocketbook and placed it on the kitchen table.

"So, *now* what do we do?" she asked, almost to herself.

Billy picked up the package and shook it again, listening to that mysterious muffled rattle.

"Why don't we open it?" he asked. "Carefully, I mean. We can see what's inside, then seal it back up so Stone will never know it's been opened."

"Ohhhh," said Veronica, shaking her head. "No, no, no. I'm not sure that's a good idea at all. I like a good mystery as much as the next guy, but this has my nerves a bit frazzled."

She glanced at her watch.

"Let's think about this," she said. "What if it's some horrible thing inside and if we know about it we'll be put in even more danger than I think we're in now!"

Billy pursed his lips.

"Okay, let's just say that *if* we open it and it's something really horrible we...well, actually I *don't* know what we'd do."

"You're a big help," laughed Veronica.

They both stared at the mysterious package for a moment or two. Billy was sitting at the table and he began drumming his fingers.

"I have similar tape in a kitchen drawer," said Veronica, looking at Billy.

"We can be very, *very* careful and not tear the paper," answered Billy, looking at Veronica.

They cautiously, slowly peeled the tape away from one end of the package and slid out a small thin cardboard box. They both sighed deeply and looked at the box, now resting on the kitchen table. They looked at each other.

"Who wants to open it?" asked Veronica.

Without answering, Billy slowly lifted the lid off the two-piece box. Cautiously, he removed a sheet of folded paper from the box, revealing a key lying on the bottom. They looked at each other. He carefully unfolded the paper. He furrowed his brow and laid the paper flat on the table. They read it. It was a handwritten list of twenty names, seventeen of which had been crossed out. They looked at the names that were remaining:

Jacob Everett
Gregory Montgomery
Mildred Winsom

?

They looked up, staring at each other.

"Now what?" asked Veronica.

"Is this some kind of hit list or what," answered Billy, equally confounded by the list. "That handwriting looks familiar. Oh, wait a minute," he said as he rushed to Alexis's room. He retrieved that small scrap of paper that had been on her nightstand. And that's where it had remained.

"Look at this," he said as he placed the scrap next to the paper from the box.

M.W. 1913 – definitely

They looked back and forth between the paper and each other's face.

"That's the same handwriting," said Billy.

"But it's not Alexis's. So, whose then?" answered Veronica.

Billy pondered this for a short minute.

"On that scrap of paper. Look. An M.W. And look at that list. A Mildred Winsom. Could that be a connection?"

Veronica bolted upright.

"And look!" she exclaimed loudly. "Jacob Everett is on that list. He's the one who shot at us at Stonehenge. Now I remember, it was *his* name in the paper. *He* was trying to kill Alexis! But now, for all intents and purposes, his name can be crossed off the list. This *must* be a hit list of some kind. But who are the good guys and who are the bad guys?"

"Okay, even *more* scary, your costar's name is on that list as well. Why? What *are* these people involved in, anyway? Jesus, Mary, and Joseph, what cat and mouse situation have *we* gotten involved with?"

"Gregory has been among the missing all this week. Claiming laryngitis. Now I wonder. This scares me. What does that number mean next to M.W.? 1913. Probably not a birthdate. If not a year, then what? An address, perhaps?

"Perhaps," answered Billy, scrunching up his face. "It might be a stretch but what's Devon's address?"

He flipped over the wrapping paper that had contained the small box.

"Hmmm. 1917 Carlingford Road. Could M.W., meaning Mildred Winsom, possibly live at 1913? I know, that sounds remote and that I might be crazy. And what about this key," he said, picking it up from the box. "It looks like a house key, perhaps."

"And what about that question mark at the bottom of the list?" asked Veronica.

"If this *is* a hit list of some kind, just perhaps there is still an unknown person that should be added. A name Alexis was hoping that Devon could supply."

"Hmmmmm," they both said at the same time.

"I think perhaps we should go to 1913 and check this out," said Billy.

"I think perhaps that's a *stupid* idea," said Veronica, placing her hands on her hips.

"Well, of course it's a stupid idea. No perhaps about it. Let's do it!" Billy exclaimed.

Veronica shook her head. Billy looked at her, arching an eyebrow.

"You really think we should, Sherlock?" she asked.

"I do, Watson. I do."

15

Gregory Montgomery had an early sexual awakening. From two unexpected sources. When he was fourteen, Darlene Sawyer, the prettiest girl in his class at school had a major crush on him. He knew it and was intrigued but a bit too timid to do anything about it. The girl was anything *but* timid. She cornered Gregory one day after school on the walk home. She lived two doors down from him on the same block in the same little town.

"My Mum and Dad aren't home from work yet, Gregory," Darlene had said coyly, "and won't be for a few more hours. Want to come in and… help me with our homework?"

Gregory was not naïve. Timid, yes, but definitely *not* naïve.

With schoolbooks and clothes askew, they fondled each other to the point of release for Gregory. These after-school sessions continued for months, until Darlene's family moved to another town.

At about that same time, Gregory discovered that he had a strange attraction to the best looking young *boy* in their class. But he was *not* going to act upon this feeling. He knew it was wrong in every sense of the word. No one should ever know. He often pleasured himself while thinking of that handsome young man, Noah Abraham.

By the time Gregory Montgomery was twenty-two, he was taking acting classes from the best drama coach in the area, David Goldman.

There was a major problem right from the start. Although he was at least two decades older, David Goldman was even more handsome than Noah Abraham. Gregory fought his impulses but they were growing stronger. He began to feel that perhaps, just *perhaps*, his coach might be having similar thoughts. Nothing was said, nothing was done, but Gregory thought that Goldman was making innocuous insinuations.

Gregory Montgomery had misinterpreted everything. He may have developed exceptional acting ability, but his young libido overruled decent sense. He made a dramatic, impulsive, and extremely inappropriate move after class one evening that changed the dynamic entirely.

Gregory approached his coach as if to ask him a question. He stood extremely close. Perhaps a bit *too* close.

"Whoa, there, Gregory," said David Goldman, grabbing Gregory's hand and slowly easing it away from his crotch and backing up. "I guess I should be flattered that such a handsome and talented young man as yourself finds me attractive. But, my boy, I don't play that game. I'm sorry that you did what you just did. I shall put the action behind us. No more will be said of this. But I hope you realize that what you might have been intending to do is strictly illegal."

Gregory could feel his anxiety climb and his face redden. He wanted to run away. Hide.

"I have to be perfectly honest with you, Mr. Montgomery," continued David Goldman, "I am not totally surprised by your actions. I've been aware of certain...shall we say telltale traits? No, no, but I *was* taken aback by the boldness of your approach. As I said, let's put this little incident behind us. You're too talented a young man. And I sincerely hope that, aside from the embarrassment of rejection, you will continue in my classes. Yes?"

Gregory was mortified. But resentment was now beginning to grow. He needed to continue the classes. He needed the coaching. He had made a wrong decision, at the wrong time, with the wrong person. Did he love David Goldman? No, of course not. Did he want to do perverted things with David Goldman? Absolutely. But he was waiting for revenge of some sort for that hasty, none-too discrete and embarrassing scene of rejection.

That time came six months later. The rest of the class had left the building and Gregory was about to walk out the door as well, when David Goldman suddenly gasped and grabbed at his chest in apparent acute pain. Gregory turned around in time to see his coach fall to the floor, gasping for breath, and sweating profusely. David Goldman was having a massive heart attack.

Gregory dropped his books and rushed to the man's side. He knelt down, leaning close to him. Instead of calling for help or assistance of any kind, Gregory leaned down and kissed the man squarely on the lips. He sat back, smiled, and watched as the poor man died right there on the floor. Gregory slowly walked out of the room.

16

Billy went to the dresser in Alexis's bedroom and retrieved the Beretta from under his boxers. Veronica went into her room and changed into a pair of wide-legged slacks. She had seen photos of Katharine Hepburn wearing similar ones and that had inspired her to go out and buy three pair in different colors. This time, when they pulled up in front of the house two doors down from Devon Stone's they didn't ask the cabbie to wait. Billy had been smoking a Lucky Strike during the cab ride, but stubbed it out on the street before walking up the steps to #1913, exhaling the last puffs of smoke as he did so.

Not really having formulated a reason for being there, they decided to play it as it came, when and if Mildred Winsom answered the door. They tried peering through the front door's stained glass windows but could see nothing. They took a deep breath and rang the doorbell. And waited. Nothing. They rang again. Nothing. They looked at each other. Billy started knocking on the door, softly at first, gaining in intensity for a minute. A taxicab pulled up to the curb in front of the house next door. The house between #1913 and Devon Stone's house. The front door of the house opened and out stepped that cantankerous old man with the rumpled grey hair. He glanced in their direction.

"What? You two again?" he shouted. "Bloody hell, what are you doing, going from door to door selling magazine subscriptions, or what?"

"Oh, so sorry, sir, but we're looking for Mildred Winsom. This *is* her address is it not?" answered Veronica, laying on the sweetness.

"It is," the man said, eyeing them suspiciously. "Nasty bitch that she is. Unfriendliest woman I've ever met. But she's not there. Just like that bloke on the other side of me. Maybe *she's* on holiday, too. Or maybe she's lying in there dead, not that I would care. You know, there *was* a murder a few houses up the street not too long ago. Never could find the bastards. Who knows? Haven't heard a peep out of that place in weeks, nor seen her come in or go out."

He started down the steps, reaching the cab and opening the door.

"Now, be gone with ya, or I'll call the constable if I see you poking around here anymore."

He got into the cab and they drove off.

"Hmmm," Billy said, as he reached into his pocket to retrieve that mysterious key. Once again, he looked up and down the street, making sure the cab had left the neighborhood and no one else was out to see what he was about to do.

Veronica held her breath as Billy inserted the key into the lock and turned it. They heard a click. He tried the knob. The door opened.

They looked at each other, their eyebrows raised in arches. Taking a quick, cautious glance up and down the street once again, they slowly eased the door open. They stepped inside, quietly closing the door behind them.

•

Mildred Winsom checked out of the third dingy cottage she'd stayed in for the past two weeks. She needed to go back home for a change of clothes. And a gun. For obvious reasons she couldn't have retrieved the gun poor Jacob was shooting when that witch, Aleksandra, killed him. She also needed desperately to speak with Gregory Montgomery.

•

"Hello?" called out Billy as they stepped cautiously into the foyer.

The receiving room to the right of the foyer had very few pieces of furniture and no carpeting so his voice practically echoed.

"Is anyone here?" he called out again, a bit louder this time. No response except for some old rattling pipes creaking somewhere in the house.

"Why are we even doing this?" asked Veronica.

"I have no idea," answered Billy, "but right now I feel like we're Nick and Nora Charles."

"Oh, I *love* that movie!" gushed Veronica with a wide smile on her face. "I want to be Myrna Loy when I grow up."

They looked around the ground floor for several minutes, discovering nothing, although they had no idea what they might even be looking for. Dirty dishes had been left in the sink in the kitchen, but they looked like they had been there for a while.

They climbed the stairs to the second floor, complete with creaking floorboards as they went. They both winced when they heard the sound but obviously no one else was around to hear it as well.

There was a small office off of the second floor hallway and Billy went in carefully.

"Ronnie, come look at this," he whispered loudly. "What do you make of it?" he asked as he held out a worn black and white photograph that he had picked up from the desk. A colorful scarf, carefully folded, was lying next to the photo.

She took the photograph, examined it for a moment and wrinkled up her nose.

"What do you think?" she asked.

The photograph was fuzzy, somewhat out of focus, and looks to have been taken with a telephoto lens. It was of a woman's face, partially in profile, with a name handwritten across the bottom followed by a large question mark. The name was Aleksandra Markarova.

•

Mildred Winsom paid the cabbie and requested that he return to get her in thirty minutes time. She tipped him well.

She went to unlock her door and was shocked to find that it was already unlocked.

I was positive I locked that before I left, she thought. *I've never been so careless.*

She stepped inside, carefully closing the door. She turned slowly around and halted. She inhaled deeply. The smell of cigarette smoke. *No one has ever smoked in this house*, she thought.

Billy and Veronica held their breaths when they heard the front door open. He peered very cautiously out of the office door, into the hallway, but couldn't see down into the foyer. He pointed and mouthed the word *"up"*, indicating that they should climb the stairs to the third floor.

Tip-toeing as they went, no floorboards squeaking this time, they reached the third landing and wondered what their next moves would be.

Billy suspected this would happen. He heard footsteps coming up from the foyer, stairs squeaking as the person climbed toward them. And, whoever it was, was getting closer.

Again, he mouthed *"up"*, and once again pointing. He hoped that the door to the rooftop wasn't locked. No squeaks on this climb either and the door *was*, indeed, unlocked.

They went out onto the rooftop and, using extreme care, silently closed the door behind them. He looked around and saw that the short walls surrounding the rooftop terrace practically abutted with the rooftop walls surrounding the terrace of house next to this one, and so on down the entire block. Two houses away was the botanical garden belonging to Devon Stone. Billy recognized it right away. The rooftop terrace they were currently on had a huge, old vegetable garden but they neither stopped to admire it nor to pick anything. There was nothing to pick anyway.

"I am so glad you're wearing those slacks and not a dress, Ronnie. Follow me. Fast!"

He leaped across the short divide between this house and the next one and, reaching back, held out his hands to help Veronica across. Just as they made it, the door swung open to the rooftop of the house they had just "invaded".

"Duck!" Billy whispered.

He waited for a few seconds and then slowly inched his head up from behind the protective wall to see who it might have been that was following them. It was a black-haired, slender woman with a mean scowl on her face. She was brandishing a pistol and appeared to know how to handle it. He was glad that he hadn't needed to use the Beretta tucked into his jacket. Not yet, anyway. She looked all around, stopped at the door to take one more visual sweep of her rooftop, then went back inside, slamming the door behind her. Billy thought he heard a click, indicating she must have locked it.

"Come on," he said, standing up, "we have one more roof to reach."

They hurried past an aviary causing a lot of nervous fluttering of wings and agitated cooing. He helped Veronica cross over another divide, and landed in the midst of Devon Stone's beautiful garden. They didn't stop to admire this one either, nor the spectacular view.

"We know that *Stone* isn't home, let's just hope that he kept his rooftop door unlocked as well."

Veronica, still trembling, agreed.

The door was, indeed, unlocked and they hastily got inside. The house was quiet and dark. *Trusting souls, these Brits,* thought Billy.

"We're good!" said Billy breathlessly.

They found the stairway leading down. They made it down two flights, not caring about any squeaking floorboards this time. Veronica kept looking around as they went.

"See? No plants. Have you seen any, Billy?"

"I wasn't looking and I don't care," he answered somewhat flippantly. "I just want to get down and get out without getting caught or shot at!"

They were about to reach the last step into the front foyer when they heard someone insert a key into the front door.

Billy muttered an obscenity, grabbed Veronica and rushed them both into the reception room off of the front hall. *Oh, no, here we go again, toots,* he thought. *Here we go again!*

They hid behind the door's archway, leaning as closely as they could up against the bookcase, and held their breaths. Again. The second time within an hour.

Slowly Billy peered around the arch, trying to see if Devon Stone had finally returned home. *No way to explain this,* he thought. But it wasn't Stone. It was that cantankerous elderly man with the rumpled grey hair from next door. Billy looked back at Veronica and she pantomimed watering and mouthed the word *"plants"*. That guy must have had a very short errand to run when he had left less than an hour ago and was now back to do his favor for his neighbor.

The man closed the door and headed past the room where Billy and Veronica were hiding and started down the hallway to the rear. He stopped a few feet down the hallway and hesitated for a moment.

Oh, no, thought Billy, he must have heard something. *We're caught now, for sure.*

Veronica closed her eyes, waiting.

The man turned to a door that was off the hallway and opened it. A strange light, almost a glow emanated from it. The man entered and they could hear footsteps going down a wooden staircase.

He's going down to a basement, they both thought simultaneously.

They waited until they could no longer hear those footsteps descending and then they made a silent but mad dash for the front door, closing it quietly behind them.

A taxicab had just pulled up to the house two doors down and they raced to it, hopping in and telling the cabbie to get the hell outta Dodge!

17

As soon as they got back in the apartment, Veronica slammed the door, locked it and secured the sliding chain door lock. Leaning up against it, she sighed loudly, and was on the verge of tears.

"I've never been so frightened in my life," she whimpered, "Not even at my first audition. What do we do now?"

"Let's look at this logically," Billy responded. "Obviously we simply can't just go to the police. What would we say? What *could* we say? We've been shot at, witnessed a murder, lied to a police officer about not knowing the shooter, and committed illegal entry regarding two houses on the same block."

"What's logical about *that*?" asked Veronica. "And which police would we go to? The ones here in London or the ones out near Stonehenge? If only Mr. Stone were around we would confront him. And if we knew how to contact Alexis we could ask her what's going on."

"Well, now that's another thing," Billy said with a shrug of his shoulders. "Who *is* Alexis? That photograph in that lady's house, what's her name...Mildred Winsom? Was that a shot of Alexis? It *sort* of looked like her but it wasn't a great shot. I remember the name scribbled across the bottom. It was, what, Aleksandra Markarova, right? Same initials as Alexis Morgan. Are we just playing games here? We figured out that M.W. was Mildred Winsom. And what about that accent? It could have been Russian and that name is definitely Russian."

Veronica headed into her bedroom.

"You certainly know how to show a girl a good time, but I hate to bring this conversation to a close. Actually, I hate that we even have to *have* this conversation but I need to be at the theater in an hour. Remember that my costar's name was on that so-called hit list. If even that's what it is. I will most definitely *not* bring that to his attention. Of course, I'm assuming that he'll even *be* on stage tonight. He's missed a lot of performances already. Which is another big mystery to me, considering his massive ego."

Billy pondered the whole big scenario and its intensity as he followed her into the bedroom.

"I should really say let's be cautious and extra vigilant but, in all honesty, who should we try to hide *from*?" he finally said. "No one has seen us or could identify us in anything we've been a part of these past few days. The guy who shot at us is in the morgue with a bullet through his brain. That old cranky guy who lives between the Stone house and the Winsom house yelled at us, twice no less, but he didn't see us do anything suspicious. Our names weren't mentioned in the newspaper regarding the murder and shoot-out at Stonehenge. So, for all intents and purposes, we're nonentities. Nobodies. Nobody knows us. Invisible, right?"

"Watch it, cowboy, now you're stepping on *my* ego."

•

Mildred Winsom anxiously paced back and forth in her kitchen. She knew almost with certainty that someone *had* been in her house. But how did they get in and who was it? And whoever he or she was, they were a smoker. The aroma must have clung to their clothing. Just about everyone in Europe was a smoker, England especially, but not her. Ever. She didn't allow anyone to smoke in her place. And, *if* anyone had gotten into her house, what were they looking for? She was also miffed because of that blasted cab driver. He hadn't returned as she had requested. Even after being handsomely tipped. *You just can't trust anyone these days*, she thought.

She went upstairs to her office. The photo of Aleksandra Markarova was still on the desk where she had left it. So was the scarf. Nothing seemed to be disturbed. She shrugged her shoulders. She thought that while she was this far upstairs she might as well go up to the roof to see if any of her late-blooming tomatoes might be ripe enough for a dinner salad. She climbed the stairs, unlocked the door to her rooftop garden and swung the door open. The crisp, fresh air felt good and she breathed deeply, trying to rid her lungs of what little cigarette smell remained. A small flock of pigeons fluttered and took flight. She slowly walked around her garden, checking this plant and that, but her plants were all wilted with nary a tomato to be had. They had been sorely neglected. She turned to go back downstairs when something caught her eye. It was on the ground, at the edge of the wall bordering her next-door neighbor's rooftop. She walked over to it, squinted at it, and bent to pick it up. Someone *had* been in her house, and up here on the roof. She seethed. It must have been an American. And, maybe worse, possibly military.

She held it and crumbled it up in her fist gritting her teeth. A half-empty pack of Lucky Strike cigarettes.

She knew that U.S. troops got Lucky Strike cigarettes in their rations. The brand's logo was stamped on each cigarette. She had heard from those in the know, that every man would flip every cigarette in the pack except for one. In that way, each time a cigarette would be lit and smoked, the stamp would burn first. Should the soldier drop his cigarette for any particular purpose, the enemy couldn't determine the country of origin from its identifying mark. The last cigarette in the pack, therefore, was the exception and should the soldier survive long enough to smoke it, it was considered lucky.

Millie held the pack firmly squeezed in her hand and screamed, in anger, at the top of her lungs.

•

Alexis Morgan had dropped off the face of the Earth. Devon Stone was still "on holiday". And now Gregory Montgomery had apparently departed the remaining run of *Private Lives*. His name had been replaced on the marquee with that of Christopher Blaze. There is always something magical about a theater. Whether it's packed to the rafters with an enthusiastic, anticipatory audience, or empty and silent after the final curtain. So many stories, onstage or off.

Veronica's performance was spot-on, giving no indication of the recent traumatic events that would, probably, have a lifetime effect on her nerves. After the evening's applause had ceased and the theater vacated, she went to her new costar's dressing room, passing a few stagehands and smiling at them as they passed. She started to knock when she thought she heard what sounded like soft sobbing. She hesitated before knocking but then tentatively did so, leaning in closer to listen.

"Go away. Please," said Christopher Blaze with a catch to his voice.

"Christopher, it's Veronica. Please. You were brilliant, as always tonight, but I noticed something in your face during curtain call. You seemed, umm, I don't know, distant, disturbed by something. Anything I can do to help?"

The door opened slowly as Christopher backed away and sat down at his makeup table. He continued removing the makeup without really turning to look at his costar.

"Christopher, I'm here for you. You know that, don't you? We've been friends as well as sparing partners on the stage. I know that you're very good friends with Gregory."

Christopher stopped what he was doing for the briefest of seconds and, without any acknowledgement, continued removing his makeup.

"Do you have any idea why he has withdrawn from this production? It was going so well and he was warmly received. Well, by all the critics except one. But *he* hates everything and everybody."

Finally there was a reaction from Christopher.

"Ha! That cold-hearted bastard of a critic loved *you*, though, Veronica, didn't he?" Christopher Blaze practically spitting out the words. "I have no idea why Clovis James is so...I don't even know what to say or call it. Venom of some sort must run through his veins. I've *never* gotten a good notice from that man. Never!"

"But the audiences love you, don't they? And that's what counts. The paying and applauding public."

Christopher sighed and pushed back in his chair. He turned to face Veronica. He cleared his throat.

"You asked a question thirty seconds ago. I shall answer it in part. Yes, Gregory and I have been friends for a long time. Very…good friends. But he and I are the polar opposites when it comes to certain things. Politics, for example. I *do* know why he withdrew. And I *do* know where he is. But I can say no more. I have given him my solemn pledge for silence. I will *not* violate our friendship or his trust. He has been treading on very dangerous, very thin ice. That ice is now quickly melting."

"I certainly won't pressure you to reveal anything further. Should I fear for *your* safety?" asked Veronica, sincerely moved, and a bit frightened, by her costar's statement.

Christopher paused for a moment.

"Frankly, I don't know how to answer that. I know this sounds so melodramatic, doesn't it? I wake up every morning thinking I'm in some Alfred Hitchcock flick. If that were the case, I'd want Rex Harrison to play me," he said laughing, which suddenly turned into a sob. "I'm sorry. I get carried away. Us theater folks are entitled, don't you agree?"

Veronica simply smiled.

"Oh, I'm sure this sounds so silly to you, doesn't it?" asked Christopher. "So removed from *your* reality. When you're not performing you and your god-awful gorgeous boyfriend probably just lollygag around all day, seeing the sights, eating bonbons, and doing whatever young lovers do."

Veronica simply smiled.

•

At approximately 3:15 A.M., Billy suddenly sat straight upright in bed. An intriguing thought had just come to him and he needed to act upon it. Not wanting to disturb a deeply sleeping Veronica, he carefully swung his feet around off the bed and padded, naked, to the telephone. He sent a telegram. Collect.

18

Devon Stone was a pen name. The name that appeared on his passport was Daniel Stein, his given name. That name was known only to a select few and rarely used.

His flight into Belgrade landed two hours late but such was the norm. He always expected it. After getting a small vehicle from the car hire lot at the airport, he drove two more hours through beautiful, rolling countryside to the small village of Rajski Konaci. He rolled the car windows down and inhaled deeply, enjoying the crisp mountain air and the aroma of farmlands. It was late in the day but he knew that someone would be waiting for him no matter the hour. He quickly checked into the quaint guesthouse in town, leaving his overnight bag in his room, and started walking briskly the two miles to his destination. Checking periodically to make certain he wasn't being followed. The moon was rising and dusk was falling quickly as he knocked on the door to a tattered old cottage, looking around as he did so. The weathered slate-roofed cottage sat on a gentle slope, backed by dense woodland. An oft-repaired rustic fence made from hand-hewn wooden posts and slats surrounded the cottage as a half dozen goats and one lone cow wandered around, paying no attention to Devon.

"Greetings, Daniel," said the wrinkled, almost decrepit man as he slowly swung the door open. "I've been waiting but, aghh, not waiting for drink. I am ahead of you. Join me."

The two men shook hands heartily as Devon stepped across the crumbling stone threshold. The man, walking hunched over from an arthritic back, led them to a couple of wooden straight-back chairs with small fluffy, soft pillows as cushions.

The cottage, with its low exposed beam ceiling, was dimly lit and smelled of the earth. Musty, musky odors combined with that of burning wood.

Devon Stone sat down in front of the fireplace that flickered and sputtered with barely a flame. The old man handed him a small glass filled with clear liquid.

They each held their glasses high.

"*Ziveli*!" said the man, raising his glass higher.

"Cheers!" Devon answered.

First inhaling the liquid's aroma deeply, the men then sipped their drinks.

"Wonderful, Luka," Devon said, calling the man by his name. "Your rakija never fails to warm the pipes on the way down. Delicious, as always."

Rakija is a potent brandy made from the distillation of various fermented fruits, apricots, apples, or grapes, depending upon who is doing the brewing. The beverage produced by Luka Petrovic, using grapes, was strong. Nearly 65% alcohol. Aside from this tantalizing drink, Luka also made Devon's favorite cheese.

"As you know," Luka began after refilling their glasses from a fancy, old, colorfully decorated flask, "I am not happy about what you and your friends are doing. I have turned an unseeing eye to...is that the right expression?"

"I believe you might mean that you turned a blind eye to what we're doing."

"Da, yes, yes. That is it," answered Luka, waving his hand. "Anyway my young friend, it is evil to kill. I know that you have been following *very* evil men. Evil men who kill. And evil women, too. As far as I know only two of them on your list remain here in Serbia. In this very town. That other Englishman, the actor, was back here again in hiding up until yesterday. He held his usual meetings. Unfortunately I believe another witch may have been murdered. No verification yet. I had kept close vigil in hopes you would arrive here in time. But he has fled once again."

Devon was not happy in hearing this.

"His time is running out, I am sure, Daniel. You are getting closer. Hopefully, my friend, *your* time is not running out. As I said, I don't like what it all means. I am torn. But my sympathies *are* with you and the others you might have helping you. Oh, how I hate all the killing," Luka said, closing his eyes and shaking his head. "But one of the witches was a relative to my late wife. She was deeply saddened and depressed by the murders. I think that is what broke her heart, weakened her and led to her death. I know I have told you all this before. Please forgive an old man for repeating. I am not giving you a lecture on what is right and what is wrong. I have seen so much. Too much. The world is not the same."

"It's never the same, Luka," said Devon sympathetically. "It seems the more civilized we've become throughout the centuries, the less civil we are becoming. A sad fact."

Luka nodded and shrugged his weary shoulders.

Devon and Luka spoke for another hour, with Luka offering a dinner of pljeskavicas, the traditional ground beef patties of Serbia, and a few stewed vegetables. Strong coffee followed.

"Beware, Daniel," Luka warned as Devon opened the door to head back to his guesthouse. "I'm sure those two blackguards must know you have arrived. Watch your step."

"Oh, I know they are aware of my presence. I saw one of the bastards at the airport in Belgrade and I'm certain I've been followed. Obviously we were too hasty in crossing their names off our list. I was extremely cautious in walking here tonight, Luka. I didn't want to be followed and put you in harm's way."

"Bah! *Koga je briga?*" Luka answered, waving it off and shrugging his bony shoulders. "Who cares, eh? I'm the last of my family. I've served my purpose. I've served you and my country well."

"I care, Luka. I care," answered Devon, giving the man a warm embrace.

Luka looked both ways when he opened his door, the landscape looked dark and foreboding. He leaned into Devon and whispered in his ear as he handed a small package to him.

"Give my regards to Chester. I believe he, too, might have an unseeing eye," he said as he slowly closed the door, then locking it.

Devon Stone, ne Daniel Stein, walked a roundabout way in returning to his guesthouse in the village with only the light from a full moon guiding the way. As he turned the corner of a dimly lit street another man started walking toward him. The man was carrying a sickle. Devon knew instinctively that this would not end well for one of them.

How obvious can one get, Devon thought to himself. *Harvesting season is long gone.*

The men kept walking toward each other. Devon was ready. He steeled his nerves.

What Devon *wasn't* ready for was when the man got closer. He threw down the sickle and withdrew a small pistol from his jacket, pointing it directly at Devon. Devon was then attacked from behind, strong arms reaching across his chest restricting his own arms in a massive, crushing bear hug. The package he was carrying dropped to the ground.

•

Mildred Winsom waited for the telephone call she was certain would soon come. The trap had been laid. It was just a matter of time. Gregory Montgomery had done his job well, played his cards perfectly. *Tit for tat,* she thought. *One of ours, one of yours. Ha! And a big one of yours at that.*

It was very early morning. The full moon shone brightly as she sat on an old wooden chair surrounded by her wilted tomato garden. She took a sip from the first cup of coffee of her day and sat back, waiting. Smiling. Gloating.

•

Devon realized in an instant that these two men were idiots.

The man holding him from behind especially knew nothing about self-defense. Devon's actions were swift. He immediately raised his feet off the ground, spreading his legs as he did so, and leaned forward, lowering his center of gravity. This threw his attacker off balance. He thrust his elbows up, releasing some of the pressure and lessening the effect of the hug. He straightened his body back up sharply, the back of his head hitting the hugger squarely in his face and breaking his nose.

Idiot number one, in the confusion of the swiftly changing scene, dropped his gun and picked up the sickle once again, rushing toward Devon. Devon's body came stomping down on the feet of the attacker behind him, making the man release him completely. Devon spun like a whirling dervish, forcefully kicking the man behind him directly in the groin and heard the man scream as he staggered backward. Devon continued spinning and, now kicking upward, the deadly tool was knocked from the hands of the man running toward him. The sickle flew straight up. It all happened in a fraction of a second. Grasping the situation, watching the deadly weapon as it slowed its ascent, Devon was deft enough and caught it by the handle as it fell back downward. Still rapidly spinning, Devon slashed the sickle across the approaching man's throat, easily severing his carotid artery and slicing through his trachea as well. Aside from a look of total shock and spurting blood, a gurgling sound was all that Devon heard as the man fell to the ground.

The bear hugger regained his footing, but not his senses. Instead of making a sensible and safe hasty retreat he came rushing at Devon once again, growling like some wild, wounded animal.

Devon was getting dizzy from all this spinning but he kept it up. He slashed the obviously very sharp sickle through the approaching man's lower abdomen, tearing through fabric and flesh. Stopping and then switching directions he continued spinning and slashed once again. Devon was fairly certain that part of an intestine of some kind followed the blade out of the man's body after the second go-round. Just to be certain, he spun and slashed one more time.

The large man stood in shock and silence for a few seconds staring into Devon's eyes and then fell to the ground, clutching his gut, letting out a mournful moan as he bled out. Devon quickly pocketed the pistol that had been foolishly thrown to the ground. He carefully placed the bloody sickle in the hand of the dead man with the gashed throat.

Not taking any more time to survey the situation, but making sure he didn't leave any traces of his being there, Devon picked up the small package that he had dropped and continued a leisurely stroll back to his guest house as his heart rate came back down to normal. It hadn't been a wasted trip after all.

When a horrified citizen came upon the grizzly scene at daybreak and notified the authorities, there was a tremendous amount of conversation and confusion as to who, actually, had killed whom.

•

Mildred Winsom had fallen asleep. Her anticipated phone call never came.

19

Two nights later, the moon was setting as a traditional London black cab, an Austin FX3, with Devon Stone as a passenger pulled up in front of his house just as another such taxicab, containing Mildred Winsom, pulled away from in front of *her* house two doors down. Neither passenger noticed the other cab nor paid any attention. The cabdriver helped Devon up the front steps with his luggage and was tipped well enough to take his wife out to dinner and the cinema the following night. She selected an American film; *The Greatest Show On Earth* and the cabbie fell asleep halfway through.

Devon waited to unpack until after he had placed his fresh supply of Manur cheese, specially wrapped to ensure its safe transport, in his refrigerator. He went up to his bedroom, removed his passport from his jacket pocket and put it securely back into his wall safe. He continued with his unpacking and then sat down on the edge of his bed as he picked up the telephone and dialed. The other phone picked up after three rings.

"Good evening, Clovis," said Devon Stone. "I'm back."

•

Billy awakened with a jolt. Waiting for Veronica to get home from this evening's performance, he was sitting in the living room listening to some relaxing music on the BBC. Perhaps *too* relaxing. He had momentarily dozed off while smoking a cigarette and an ash had just dropped onto his leg and burnt a small hole in his pants. He swatted at his leg and extinguished his Lucky Strike. *Lucky I didn't burn the place down*, he thought. He leaned back in his chair when there came a loud knocking on the door to the apartment. A *shave and a haircut two bits* kind of knock. He glanced at his watch and then frowned. He hastily retrieved his Beretta from the bedroom and went up to the door. The knock came again, louder this time. He hesitated for a few seconds before unlocking everything. Grabbing the knob, he thrust open the door, pistol ready.

"Surprise!" yelled Peyton Chase, arms outstretched.

"What the…?" said a dumbfounded Billy, mouth agape. He quickly stuffed the Beretta into his pants pocket. And he just stood there staring.

"What, no hugs and kisses? No 'what a nice surprise?' No 'come on in, buddy, glad to see ya?' And after twenty friggin' hours on a rattletrap of a plane, too. Gee whiz, pal, I'm disappointed," Peyton said, barely controlling his laughter.

"Well, yeah, buddy, get your ass in here," said a smiling Billy, taking Peyton's hand and shaking it firmly. They patted each other on their backs. Peyton picked up his big duffle bag and followed Billy into the apartment.

"Okay, not that I'm *not* glad to see you, because I am, but why are you here?"

"Your telegram did it, even if it *was* sent collect. Cheap bastard," Peyton answered with a grin.

"Sorry about that, I'll reimburse you for it. Promise. I sent it late at night from here in the apartment. I had that brilliant idea and felt like it couldn't wait until I could get to a Western Union office. Please, sit. You must be exhausted after that flight. You want a beer or something?"

"Thought you'd never ask, pal. What's the 'something'?"

"Gin. Bourbon. Rye. Scotch."

"You running a bar here, or what?" Peyton snickered. "Just surprise me. I'm easy."

Billy went into the kitchen and brought out a half-empty bottle of Tullamore D.E.W. Irish whiskey along with two shot glasses.

They toasted to each other's health. Three times.

"Okay, back to my original question but…hey, if you're *here*, who's minding the store?"

"Don't worry about it. I put a big *Gone fishing-Back in a month* sign in the window and locked the place up."

"Are you crazy? Hunting season is just beginning. These will be our best months!" said an incredulous Billy.

"Well, there is obviously a hunting season going on now over on *this* side of the pond, my friend. And the game ain't deer or pheasants or grouse or what have you. From what I've learned, the targets are human. Female. And Russian."

Billy frowned. He was confused.

"Whether or not *you're* mixed up in it yet, I haven't determined," said a now-serious Peyton. "But you sent a name for me to check out."

"And?"

"Sit back. Relax. I was able to find out only a very small bit, but enough of a bit for me to decide to hightail it over here and help you. If I can."

"What did you find out?"

Peyton sighed deeply.

"Remember crazy Walter Leach from high school?"

"Wasn't he the one with those inch thick glasses and always had his nose in one book or another, and had awful acne and b.o.?"

"Yeah, that's the one. Anyway, during the war he worked in the OSS. After it was disbanded he went over to the CIA. I called in a favor or two."

"What are you talking about? What favors?"

"Before we left to come fight over here in that little old war, I hooked him up with loosey-goosey Lucy. You remember, the chick I banged in high school, right? Who knew, eh? They hit it off right from the start. They now have three kids and a house just outside of D.C. somewhere. But I'm getting off the point. Crazy old Walter has some good friends over here in MI6."

Billy's mouth hung open, his eyes wide.

"They could say very little and I really mean *very* little, because there is something big in the works. Have *no* idea what it might be at this time. But I *did* find out about that name you sent to me. Aleksandra Markarova."

"Could she actually really be Veronica's roommate, Alexis Morgan?"

"I doubt it, pal. Not unless she's come back from the grave. Aleksandra Markarova has been dead for well over a year. She was murdered."

•

Having met Peyton Chase alongside Billy at one of her USO shows during the war, no introductions were needed. But Veronica, too, had been surprised by his sudden appearance. She was drained following a two-performance day on stage, but she sat and chatted with both men for an hour or so before heading off to bed. She placed fresh sheets on the bed in Alexis's room and bade them both a goodnight.

The following morning, as all three sat in the kitchen sharing a pot of strong coffee and downing a few muffins, her telephone rang. She glanced at the clock on the wall. 8:35. *What now?* she thought to herself as she picked up the receiver.

"Good morning, Miss Barron," said a deep voice. "I hope I haven't awakened you from your beauty sleep too early. This is Devon Stone and I've been told that you have a package that is of interest to me."

20

Knowing that she had an evening performance to get to, Devon Stone invited Veronica to stop by with the package for a late afternoon cocktail hour. Billy said that he would go with her for "protection" (from *what*, he wasn't sure), and Peyton said he would go to protect them both. Just in case. Both men would be carrying concealed weapons. Peyton had brought a small arsenal with him from the States in his large duffle bag and he selected his favorite, a Browning Hi-Power. *Just in case.*

The cab with the three of them pulled up in from of the Stone residence and, with trepidation, they got out. They stood there for a moment, as if not sure what to do next. Or what to expect.

"Let's go, cowboys," Veronica said, leading the way up the stairs.

Devon Stone opened the door and was momentarily taken aback by seeing three people there and not just Veronica.

"Well, I guess I *should* have baked that cake," he laughed. "Come on in. The gin is cold and the ice is melting."

He ushered them into the foyer, giving Veronica a sweet kiss on both cheeks.

"Billy Bennett, how nice to see you again. I was sure by now you had returned home to the colonies," he said with a grin.

"Wow, I'm impressed Mr. Stone. You remembered my name."

"Oh, Mr. Bennett, you have no idea what I can remember. And this gentleman is...?"

Peyton extended his hand shaking Stone's hand firmly and vigorously.

"I'm Peyton Chase, Mr. Stone, a good friend of Billy's. And his business partner as well. I popped over last night for an unexpected visit."

"A pleasure meeting you and, please, all of you, let's forego the mister stuff, alright? Come with me."

He turned and walked into the reception room to the left of the foyer. The one where Veronica and Billy had hidden when that cantankerous old guy from next door came to water the plants. The two of them exchanged quick glances and Billy gave her a wink.

"As I said, the gin is cold. Would you all care for a refreshing gin and tonic? Or would something else be to your liking?"

They all nodded in unison.

"No, that would be fine, mister...er, Devon. Gin sounds great," answered Veronica. "Of course, I probably shouldn't speak for my two companions."

"No, that's fine, Devon. Sounds great to me," said Billy, with Peyton nodding right beside him.

He fixed them all a drink, adding a squeeze of fresh lime into each one and garnishing the glasses with a slice of the green citrus.

"Cheers! Here's to your fabulous performance, Veronica," said Stone with a wide smile.

To which performance is he referring, she thought to herself. *The one onstage or the one now, where I'm pretending that I'm not so nervous I may pass out?*

"My parents and I were touring the States way back in 1931, when I was just a mere innocent lad of twenty-five. They took me to the original Broadway production of *Private Lives* with Noel Coward and Gertrude Lawrence in the leads, believe it or not. Of course I was too young and naïve to appreciate what a classic it would become but after seeing you in the role of Amanda I simply cannot believe that Gertrude was any better than you, my dear."

Now I may pass out from that lavish praise, thought Veronica.

"Oh, Devon. No, no, no, you are way too kind. I must be blushing from head to toe. Thank you. When did you see *our* show?"

Without hesitation he answered.

"On Saturday, September the 27th. The curtain was held for twenty-three minutes while awaiting the arrival of a young American cinema star. That was Elizabeth Taylor. She happens to be in England, I believe, promoting her newly released film *Ivanhoe*. God help us all! Sir Walter Scott is no doubt doing frantic, angry cartwheels in his grave. Anyway, that was a few nights after we all met at my party here. When you both departed without saying goodnight," and Devon smiled broadly, arching one eyebrow.

"And, while we're on that subject," Devon said, toning down his smile, "I believe your ex-roommate gave something to you, right?"

Veronica swallowed deeply. She was certain that her armpits might be getting a bit damp. She reached into her purse.

"Yes, Alexis said to make sure you got this." And she nervously handed the package to Devon.

"Thank you, I appreciate the safety in which you kept it, Veronica."

He started to put it down on a table at the far end of the room when he stopped. He looked at the package, flipping it over and over in his hands. He looked at one end and then the other. He closed his eyes and chuckled softly.

"Hmmm…" he said, looking directly at Veronica. "By any chance, did curiosity get the better of you, my dear?"

Veronica, again, swallowed deeply and she was almost certain that everyone in the room could hear her heartbeat.

"And if…," she started to say, her nerves about to shatter, "we happened to take a quick teensy-weensy tiny peek at what was inside, what would happen?"

"Oh, my. That would be a pity," answered Stone, again without hesitation. "Then I'd have to kill you all!"

The look of panic swept across the faces of the three Americans in the room. The two men were too momentarily shocked by that statement to reach for their weapons. Devon Stone started laughing convulsively.

"Relax, Yanks, relax. I'm just pulling your legs, as the expression goes. But, in all honesty, that *does* put a different wrinkle in the fabric. Up to this point you were merely couriers delivering an innocent package. Unwittingly, you've become participants."

"Participants in what?" asked Billy.

"Well, in one respect, you were already participants, weren't you, now that I think about it? You witnessed a murder and, as far as I know, you didn't supply any information to the police identifying a certain female as the perpetrator. Am I correct?"

Both Billy and Veronica nodded in agreement. Peyton just sat there, innocently sipping his gin and tonic.

"And as far as that young lady is concerned…" he walked over the door on the far side of the room. The door in which Alexis, and then Little Min, had entered the night of the party. He opened the door. "You may as well come out now, my dear. I think we've confused these poor souls and now they have gotten themselves involved. A bit *too* involved but nevertheless. Actually, we may be able to use them to our advantage."

Billy, Veronica and Peyton exchanged quick, confused glances.

"Alexis!" shouted Veronica. "Oh, my god, you're safe and sound. I was *so* worried about you. Well, *whoever* you might really be."

"Obviously you're *not* Aleksandra Markarova, now, are you?" asked Billy, looking back and forth between the young lady and Devon Stone.

"No," she answered sadly, "unfortunately I am not Aleksandra. I am Anoushka Markarova. Her younger sister. We bear a striking resemblance."

"Was Aleksandra one of the witches?" asked Peyton, causing Billy's and Veronica's heads to suddenly jerk around to stare at him in further confusion and disbelief.

"Yes," Anoushka answered as a tear rolled down her cheek. "She was one of the murdered ones."

"Ah, ha!" shouted Peyton jumping up and nearly spilling his drink. "I've done my homework, buddy," he said as he turned to Billy. "I started putting the pieces together and you are *not* going to believe this."

"Okay," said Billy with a dazed look on his face. "Can I assume that we're *not* talking about something like Halloween or Salem…or Macbeth witches?"

Veronica almost looked catatonic.

It was time for Devon to take over.

"You may, indeed, make that assumption, Billy. Let me fix you all another drink. I shall tell this tale and it may take a while. I'll make sure, though, Veronica, that you make your curtain time."

21

"Obviously things are a little more complicated with you three now involved...and trust me, like it or not, you *are* now involved. You unwittingly did it to yourselves. But, then again, in all honesty both Anoushka and I started you on the path when we decided that you two should be roommates."

Veronica shook her head in confusion, putting her hands to her temples.

"I'm sorry," she said, "but somewhere from the beginning of your last sentence to the end of it my mind went blank. In theater-speak, I need clarification of that line reading."

Devon chuckled and walked over to the door of the room that had produced Anoushka a few minutes before and opened it.

"You may as well come out here, too, Clovis. In theater-speak, we need the entire cast on stage."

He had used air quotes when he said *theater-speak*.

Now Veronica was even more confused and rattled than she was a second ago. Billy stood up. Peyton just sat there swirling the remainder of his drink in his glass.

Slowly, tentatively, Clovis James came out of the room. Veronica stared at him.

"*You're* Clovis James? *The* Clovis James? The theater critic who spews hurtful, ego-damaging, sarcastic criticisms from behind his typewriter?"

"Yes, Miss Barron. One and the same." And he smiled broadly, even giving her a slight bow.

She folded her arms across her chest and pursed her lips.

"I don't know whether I should kiss you for your extremely kind review of my performance or slap you soundly across your face for your bashing of my costar. He is brilliant in that role."

"Yes. He is, I have to admit," answered the critic, "And, yes, he's a fine actor in *every* respect. And you will soon discover how fine an actor the scoundrel really is."

"Okay," said Devon as he tried to take control of the conversation once again. "Please let me get back to the dire situation at hand. We're wasting time if we resort to petty bickering about theater critiques and Veronica has to be onstage a few short hours away. Apparently your friend here, Mr. Chase, knows at least *some* aspect about the topic at hand. Right, sir?" indicating Peyton who suddenly looked up.

"Well, I know about the witches but I don't know much about the murders. I could find out only a fraction of a tidbit from a friend of a friend at MI6."

"Ah, MI6," said Devon, nodding his head. "Yes, I too, have a friend at MI6. A very close friend. Well, allow me to bring the situation into focus with some of the details your friend of a friend left out. But let me make one thing very clear, this has nothing to do with hocus-pocus or witchcraft in any way."

And Devon Stone began his clarification.

22

"This is certainly going to sound like a major history lesson, my friends, which of course, it is. But you need to know what has happened so you can understand what we," Devon said, pointing to Anoushka and Clovis, "are doing. Between 1939 and 1941, Nazi Germany and the Soviet Union were allies, with Stalin providing extremely substantial support to Nazi Germany. For some reason the alliance crumbled and Hitler being Hitler initiated Operation Barbarossa on June 22, 1941, the invasion of the Soviet Union by Nazi Germany. Within the year Hitler's troops had advanced almost one thousand miles to within shooting distance of Moscow. Mobile killing units succeeded in the mass murder of Soviet Jews, Soviet prisoners of war, and innocent Soviet civilians. Millions of them."

Devon paused to take a breath, a deep sigh, and a sip from his drink.

"At that time," he continued, "women in the Soviet Union were barred from combat. However, a very wise Major used her shrewd mind and position to persuade Stalin to form all-female combat units. About one of these units, the all-female 588th Night Bomber Regiment, is what you really need to know."

The three Americans sat in rapt awe as they listened.

"This very brave (and often reckless) regiment of female Russian pilots flew over thirty-thousand missions fighting against the Nazi regime. These daredevils flew in rickety, old, and very noisy wood and canvas Polikarpov U-2 biplanes, originally used for training purposes only, dating from 1928. Every night, well after dark, these women would fly to their intended targets over the Nazi-occupied territory of the Soviet Union and then, shutting off or idling their noisy engines, make a silent dive, with only the wind noise to indicate their presence. Their bombs would then be released and their engines restarted to fly quickly away. With open cockpits, the women had to contend with the freezing cold as well as the bullets from their intended targets."

Veronica noticed that tears were welling up in Anoushka's eyes.

"To the Germans," Devon continued on, "the almost silent wind sound of the diving planes reminded them of the sound of broomsticks. A witch's broomstick, obviously. And hence, these pilots became known as the Night Witches. *Die Nachthexen*, in German. The German pilots both hated and feared the Night Witches, and any German pilot who shot one down was automatically awarded an Iron Cross."

Devon Stone did not include every little detail regarding the Night Witches, thinking it unnecessary and confusing to the trio. He paused to take another sip of his gin and tonic.

"My sister, Aleksandra," spoke up Anoushka, taking advantage of the momentary silence, "was one of those very brave women. We say *Nochnyye Vedmy* in Russian, or as you say in English, Night Witches. Sometimes the trigger release for the bombs that her plane carried would become stuck and she would risk her life even more by climbing out onto the wing to fix it so the bombs could drop."

Then *she* paused as the tears began to flow down her cheeks.

Billy, Veronica, and Peyton sat silent, barely breathing, knowing that there was much more to this story. Something that spans the gap between 1945 and 1952.

Devon sighed deeply, clenching and unclenching his fists as he paced back and forth continuing his story.

"Unfortunately, for some Nazi-sympathizers the German surrender, twice, you might recall, did not bring World War II to an end. Their hatred continues to this very day. This, lady and gentlemen," nodding first to Veronica and then to Billy and Peyton, "is what all this sinister activity is about. Those of us who care about peace and prosperity were unaware for a few years about murders being conducted surreptitiously, mostly in the Soviet Union, but elsewhere across Europe as well. One by one the surviving Night Witches were being tracked down, targeted and murdered, probably out of pure hated and revenge."

"I am an avid reader," Anoushka interrupted, "mystery books, especially. I read Agatha Christie's *And Then There Were None* and Devon Stone's *The Fallen*, both books about revenge murders. I had a discomforting feeling something sinister was happening regarding my sister's death and those other brave women who flew with her. I was able to get in contact with Devon and he was intrigued enough to start an investigation with some other associates of his."

The three Americans exchanged glances and shared a single thought. *Our host*, they were thinking, *is one among many who is then targeting those murderers.*

"With the help of various intelligence agencies, MI6 included naturally, we have been able to isolate these dangerous, murderous individuals."

"Who are this *we*, Devon?" asked Veronica.

"A group of us patriotic souls who appreciate what the witches did to help win the war, my dear. There were twelve of us originally but the other side was shrewd enough to figure out what we were doing and it has a hit list. There are only three of us left to fight now. Clovis, Anoushka, and yours truly."

"Let me guess," interrupted Billy. "In simple terms, you and your compatriots are murdering the murderers."

"Semantics, Mr. Bennett. Merely semantics," responded Devon Stone. "We prefer to think that we're eradicating a deadly disease. A disease called hatred. A disease called prejudice. We're not so naïve to think that this will end with us. It will still exist. It may even grow in time. There will be many more such events still ahead, as there have been for the millenniums behind us. We're taking it one situation at a time."

"Be that as it may be, Devon, can we assume that this list that Veronica and I sneakily *peeked* at was, indeed, *your*....hmmm...hit list?"

"Again, semantics, dear boy. But that is an axiom that surely cannot be refuted."

"I have absolutely *no* idea what you just said, Devon, but can we take that as a yes?" asked a confused looking Peyton.

Devon chuckled.

"To answer you succinctly, yes. The names crossed off that list have... well, let's just say that they have gone on to reconnect with their ancestors."

"But, aren't *those* murders then being investigated by the police somewhere?" asked Veronica. "Surely that would attract *somebody's* attention."

"Oh, we are *extremely* cautious about that, young lady," answered Devon. "We try, in most instances, to make sure that every detail is worked out in advance once we identify our intended target. Of course, extenuating circumstances could intervene. Say, if we're attacked by surprise in an ambush. Doing research for all of my books, I have discovered *so* many ways of doing certain things to a person. We make their demise look like a horrible accident, or a suicide, *or* we get rid of the body in such a way that he or she simply becomes a missing person and not a murdered one. And, by the by, those individuals attached to those names came from various parts of Europe. Oh, sorry, one was even from the good old U.S. of A. Our very adept critic here, Mr. James, tracked down that scoundrel on his recent trip to Manhattan."

"Right," Clovis James said, picking up the story. "He had been under my surveillance for a few days, never suspecting a thing, I can only assume. I followed the bloody bloke down into the Grand Central subway station. It was rush hour and the platform was packed. Commuters eager to get home were shoving and pushing. New Yorkers can be so *horribly* rude. Obviously the poor man I was following must have been *so* terribly clumsy, tripping like that and falling off the platform in front of the oncoming

#7 train. I couldn't believe how easy it was. Quite a commotion ensued, as you can imagine. Walking a few short blocks away, I whistled a happy tune as I strolled into the St. James Theater an hour or so later to watch Yul Brynner in *The King and I*."

Devon rolled his eyes and shook his head. Veronica, Billy, and Peyton reacted with their mouths agape.

"And," Devon Stone started in again, "number seven on our list, thanks to lovely French-speaking Anoushka here, was treated to a rather unique view from atop the Eiffel Tower a couple months ago. I'm sure he enjoyed it all the way down. Well, he *did* have to make an abrupt stop on the first floor. Frenchmen fall *so* easily for flirtatious young things," he said with a wink. "I found that terribly ironic, actually. During the German occupation of Paris in 1940 Hitler ordered that the tower be destroyed. Along with the entire city, for that matter. Fortunately neither happened."

Again the three Americans sat stunned into silence. Veronica and Billy shared a fleeting, brief memory. What were the chances? Slim to none. Maybe. There have been *many* suicide jumpers from the Eiffel Tower.

"Please don't feel compelled to comment," Devon said sarcastically adding a wink, as he stared into their shocked, silent faces.

Peyton downed his drink.

"Be that as it may," Devon started yet again, "continuing where I left off before being interrupted by the cold-hearted critic. There was a hotbed of Nazi-lovers in Serbia but also a very large resistance group there. I have made a few trips back and forth between here and there recently. This is becoming more and more difficult and frustrating, as we seem to be closing in on the last few names on that list. But I remain very optimistic. *A pessimist sees difficulty in every opportunity. An optimist sees the opportunity in every difficulty.*"

"Was that a quote from one of your books or something?" asked Billy smugly.

Devon Stone smiled and shook his head.

"No. No, my boy. That was spoken by our beloved Winston Churchill. I long for his wisdom and his choice of just the right words at just the right time."

There was a brief silence in the room.

"To continue, once again, the names remaining on our list are Brits. Since you first saw that list, you must now know that our sharpshooter here, Miss Markarova, eliminated a rather nasty fellow by the name of Jacob Everett. He was a brutal killer and you both were very lucky that she came prepared. There are two other names remaining to be dealt with and one unknown entity. We have no idea yet whether we are searching for another male or female. Whoever that person may be is extremely cunning and shrewd. He or she is flying under the radar at the present time. *Way* under. That elusive person did their dirty work right here in London, killing two of our people. Anoushka had just recently confirmed that Mildred Winsom was definitely one of the Nazi-sympathizers here in London. She narrowly escaped from Winsom after the woman thought she was actually Aleksandra. She lost a scarf of hers in the struggle before she managed to get away. Fearing that one or more of those killers were quickly closing in on *her*, Anoushka contacted you and gave you that package. She was afraid that she might not survive to get it to me. That was during the short time that I had gone to Serbia thinking that Gregory Montgomery was hiding out there. My intent was to eliminate him there. Up till then I wasn't aware of Winsom. We do know now that Mildred Winsom is a particularly vicious killer, quite often beheading her victims."

23

"Oh," gasped Veronica. "Mildred Winsom lives two doors from this very house!"

"As I just said, we didn't have a name to attach to that assassin until just recently. My close friend in MI6 alerted me once her identity was figured out. Coincidence that she resides close by? We can only assume so, although assumptions can be deadly. Wait. How did you--? Ohhh, that list you *peeked* at. So you were able to figure that out, Sherlock and Watson, eh?"

"We prefer Nick and Nora," said Billy matter-of-factly.

"Excuse me?" Devon said in confusion.

"Never mind. No importance. But she wasn't home anyway."

He regretted saying that the moment it left his lips.

Devon stared back and forth between Veronica and Billy, shaking his head. He rattled the small box containing the hit list and key. Anoushka had obtained that key from a trusted friend with very special talents and certain connections.

"Please don't tell me that you went into her house," he finally said.

Veronica and Billy sat perfectly still, hardly breathing, looking up at the ceiling, and making no eye contact.

"Bloody hell", said Devon, "You went in. To her house."

"Well, we came right back out again," said Veronica trying to sound innocent, neglecting to tell the rest of their visit and narrow rooftop escape that ended in this very house. In this very room.

"And what did you expect to find?" asked Devon, perhaps a bit too loudly.

"Well, we didn't know," responded an embarrassed Billy contritely. "That's why we came right back out again."

"Really? How then, were you able to find out the name to Anoushka's sister, thinking her to be Alexis?"

•

There was much more story remaining for Devon to tell, but Veronica needed to get to the theater in time for the evening's performance. Before leaving, he admonished the trio to be vigilant. Not that they would be connected to this deadly cat and mouse game by the assassins but, in this case, one shouldn't make those deadly assumptions. At this point, both sides in this game had targets on their backs.

He watched as the taxicab pulled away from the curb. Closing the door, he returned to the reception room, asking if either Clovis or Anoushka needed their drinks refreshed. They did, with each one requesting that Devon omit the tonic this time.

"Could those three really be in harm's way now?" asked Clovis James.

"Oh, it's possible," answered Devon. "A remote possibility, I suppose, but it *is* lurking there. The remaining assassins have bigger fish to fry at the moment…meaning *us* three. The info that I received about the possibility of Gregory Montgomery hiding out in that conclave in Serbia proved to be false. Well, sort of. He *had* been there but then departed for further points unknown. I am more than convinced that he was the one who dispatched poor Little Min. As we've since learned, that was his modus operandi and she was the one of us who had cleverly identified him as one of the evildoers."

"So," started Anoushka, "it is basically down to us three to find and eliminate the *remaining* three. Two identities we know. One more we do not."

"That, basically, is it," agreed Devon. "You make it sound so simple," he said with a wink.

"What about your friendly neighborhood police Inspector?" asked Clovis. "Has Vanderhoff had any luck with his investigation regarding Little Min? We, of course, *think* we know who the perpetrator was, but has he just let the case linger?"

"He calls from time to time," answered Devon, fixing himself a third drink…adding the tonic. "I think he's flummoxed by the case and just keeps calling to appease me. He would probably have a coronary if he ever found out about *our* activities, wouldn't he?"

And all three laughed.

"Not wanting to make light of this bloody mess in any way," said Clovis, sipping his gin, "but considering your actual profession, Stone, can we expect a book about this from you when this is all over? Should you survive, that is?"

Devon laughed and rolled his eyes.

"Oh, I have no doubt a book will come from this."

•

And Then There Were None, the Agatha Christie book to which Anoushka Markarova referred, dealt with a criminal judge with a very strong sense of justice coupled with an unbridled bloodlust. He sentenced murderers to death upon being found guilty following their respective trials but then put a very murderous scheme into play with those he felt had escaped justice.

Devon Stone's recent book, *The Fallen*, had a young woman as its protagonist seeking revenge for the rape and subsequent murder of her twin sister by a group of her fellow university students.

Neither book, however, ended well for the person seeking revenge and justice.

24

"I don't feel good about this thing that Devon and his friends are doing," said Veronica as the cab pulled away from Stone's house. "It's just not right. Not right at *all*. They are nothing but vigilantes. Cold-blooded vigilantes at that! Vengeance is mine, saith the Lord. They're taking things into their own hands. They are acting as judge and jury."

"Ronnie," said Billy after a short silence, "I know that you're a believer. And I'm okay with that. You know that I'm *not* a believer and, as far as I can tell, you're okay with that, too. Sooner or later….much, *much* later I hope…we'll each find out the truth, one way or the other. One of us will be surprised. One of us will be disappointed."

"Amen, brother!" laughed Peyton. Billy shot him a look.

"Murder is murder, you're absolutely right, Ronnie," continued Billy. "Can what Devon and the others are doing be justified? Could they really be exonerated in a court of law? Hmmm…tough call there. But I *seriously* doubt it. Me? I find no fault whatsoever in their endeavors to rid the Nazi-loving vipers. None whatsoever. If you had seen firsthand some of the atrocities that were committed perhaps you wouldn't be so swift to judge."

The rest of the ride through the streets of London was a silent one.

Veronica exited the taxicab at the theater, kissing Billy goodbye, and hurried into the stage door entrance. Billy gave the address to Veronica's apartment building to the cabbie and sat back turning to look Peyton squarely in the eye.

"So, what do you think?" he asked.

"I think that spunky Anoushka is the hottest chick I've seen in some time. Wonder how she feels about American guys?"

"Jesus, man! Keep it in your pants, buddy. That's *not* what I meant. Now what?" Billy continued, unfazed by Peyton's response. "Despite what Stone said, I think we just *might* end up in someone's crosshairs. What do you think?"

"What do I think? I think I'm glad that I packed all that I did when I came here," answered Peyton. "I told you I felt it was hunting season over here. And now I think we need to go hunting."

•

Even though he had tried to assuage their fears, Veronica was so distraught by what Devon Stone had told them that she missed a cue. Being the ultimate professional that he was, Christopher Blaze quickly covered up for her with an ad-lib, drawing an unscripted laugh from the unknowing audience. His ego was stroked. Gregory Montgomery was still amongst the missing and she would surely recognize him if she glanced out into the audience during curtain call. But she had no idea what that dangerous Mildred Winsom looked like. Could *she* be sitting out there somewhere, staring up at her next victim on stage, waiting to strike?

•

"What the *hell* were you expecting when you packed to come here, World War Three?" Billy exclaimed as he stared into Peyton's large duffle bag, now spread open on the floor.

One by one, he pulled the rifles out of the bag, held them up and examined them.

"A Marlin 336? We're not going after deer, you know," he chuckled. "Okay, I get the Winchester 70. Certainly can't beat it for accuracy, or this one, the Savage 99. Good choices, I guess. None of them are classified as Nazi-hunting but...oh, wait!" he suddenly said as he picked up the fourth rifle from the duffle. "Oh, wow. Haven't seen one of these for a couple of years. Was this one in our shop?"

"Not before you left to come over here," answered Peyton. "I saw it in a catalogue and just knew we needed it in our place. If just for a conversation starter among our customers. She's a beauty, ain't she?"

Billy whistled a low whistle through his teeth as he examined the Sturmgewehr 44, otherwise known at the StG44. A German assault rifle. With deadly precision and accuracy.

"I brought it along, really, just to show it off to you. But it's kinda ironic, isn't it? A German rifle to hunt down Nazi-loving sympathizers? Won't that be a kicker! I got the ammo for all stuff in there, too, you know. Don't forget those sidearms that we both have. We're ready to go, pal. Oh, did you see that other surprise way down at the bottom?"

Billy leaned over and fumbled around all the boxes of ammunition and pulled out one more weapon. Although he wasn't terribly sure what either he or Peyton could do with it. Or why. But it sure was beautiful.

"This has been in that front display case of ours for a couple years, right?" asked Billy as he held up the knife.

"Yep, sure has. Guys have looked at it but never made an offer. I thought what the heck."

It was, indeed, beautiful. A Marbles Gladstone Michigan knife, complete with a leather sheath. The knife was almost 9" long and Billy could tell that it had been recently sharpened.

"Should we share what we have here with Stone or keep quiet about it for now?" asked Billy.

"We might never even need any of this stuff, pal, so I'd say keep it on the Q.T. for now," Peyton answered, with a slight shrug of his shoulders. "Perhaps even from Veronica. If it were up to me, I wouldn't want to scare her any more than I think she already is. I'm hoping we just put all this stuff back into our inventory when we get back home. I assume that you *are* planning on coming back home, right?"

"Frankly, I should have been back home weeks ago. I was planning on being here for one stinking week. A little murder or two changed those plans in a damn hurry. Ronnie and I got dragged into this and then I stupidly went and got *you* involved. The frickin' situation sure got out of hand in a hurry, if you ask me…which, of course, you didn't."

The two men sat down on the side of the bed, side by side. They each sighed.

"You know, buddy," Billy said to his friend, "You can just play it safe and head back home. This really isn't *your* mess, actually, any more than it is ours. Although I think *we're* here until it's resolved. But, please, probably for your own safety you should just pack up your arsenal and have Pan Am carry you safely back to Idlewild."

"Billy," said Peyton, turning to look at his friend. "You and I went through Hell and back in the sky and on the ground a few years ago. Well, more than a few, but you know what I mean. We fought well together. We got banged up a bit together. We came through it together. We'll come through this together as well. And we can reward each other with a Medal of Honor…or at least a scotch or two."

25

"Are you two *nuts?*" asked an incredulous Veronica as she stared into Peyton's duffle bag. "This is insane! You can't just come over here, loaded for bear, and start killing people, no matter how evil they might be."

"Hmm, that's funny, because that's just what we did a few years ago," answered Billy, crossing his arms across his chest. "Only this time we won't be in uniform."

"That was different," responded a now angry Veronica. "*Totally* different. That was wartime."

"Devon told us the war hasn't ended for some deranged people, Veronica, and he's simply trying to help them see the error in their judgment."

Peyton snickered at that last part.

They had not intended for Veronica to see their arsenal. She had quietly entered the flat, arriving late from the theater, not wanting to disturb either man if they were sleeping. Instead, she heard them chattering away in Peyton's bedroom. She went in to say goodnight and stopped dead in her tracks when she saw the open duffle bag.

"Besides," she persisted, "this is *not* your battle, Billy. Nor *yours*, Peyton! Hopefully those people that Devon and his friends are after haven't a clue about our very existence. Hopefully. I know I said that already. But I'll repeat it again. Hopefully. I'm a nervous wreck about this situation. I am very fond of Alexis...well, I mean Anoushka...and although things were fine beforehand, I wish, now that I never invited her to live here. I know that must have been manipulated somehow by Devon or Clovis James. They obviously wanted to see if I could find out something, or *anything*, from Gregory Montgomery. Oh, damn, this has become such a tangled mess, hasn't it?"

Her telephone ringing broke the momentary silence. It made all three of them jump.

She glanced at her watch. 12:25 A.M. They exchanged nervous glances as she picked up the receiver.

"Hello? Excuse me? Oh. Oh, yes. Yes, he *is* here. Just a minute, please." She handed the phone to Peyton with a confused look on her face and a concerned look on his.

Billy and Veronica stepped back and looked at each other, Billy shrugging his shoulders.

With his back to them, Peyton was listening to the calling party. His normally erect body suddenly went limp, his shoulders drooping, along with his head. He said something that couldn't be heard and he hung up the phone.

"That was my father," Peyton said sadly as he returned to them. "When I first got here I sent them a telegram with your address and phone number just in case they needed to reach me for any particular reason. My Mom hasn't been well and I wanted them to be able to call me if necessary. She had a heart attack three hours ago. It was massive…and fatal. I'm sorry but I have to go home."

Veronica rushed to his side and hugged him strongly as the man sobbed.

•

Leaving his arsenal behind, with the exception of his beloved Browning Hi-Power, Peyton was headed to the London Airport fifteen minutes after his upsetting phone call. Whatever flight might be headed back to the

U.S. was his goal. But he knew the chances of very early morning flights westbound were slim.

———————————

It was matinee day, meaning that Billy had hours to spend alone. So, after sleeping late and sharing an early light lunch together while commiserating over Peyton's loss, Billy set out to play tourist.

He wasn't apprehensive about wandering the streets. As far as he knew, the people who were stalking Devon Stone and his friends didn't have a clue about him and Veronica. He carried his Beretta, well concealed, just in case, but he felt confident regarding his safety.

He wandered through the sprawling London Tower, picking up bits and pieces of information from the Beefeater guides as he passed other groups of tourists and stood totally impressed by the display of the crown jewels. Noticing several large black crows perched on fence railings as he walked around the grounds, he asked about them. He didn't remember seeing birds like these anywhere else throughout the city.

"Ah, yes, the ravens," answered one of the guides, a Yeoman Warder. "Very important indeed. Our Ravenmaster keeps at least six of these beauties around the tower at all times. We are of the belief that if the ravens depart, the kingdom will fall. Superstition of course but, nevertheless…" and he chuckled, shrugging his shoulders.

Billy's leisurely stroll then took him across the beautiful old Tower Bridge, stopping midway to watch boats glide slowly up and down the Thames. He began to notice signs posted along the way advertising various forms of fireworks. He lit a cigarette as he studied one with curiosity.

Standard FIREWORKS

HUDDERSFIELD, ENGLAND

TO GET THE BEST RESULTS ALWAYS FOLLOW THE
DIRECTIONS MARKED ON THE FIREWORKS

HERE ARE A FEW GOOD TIPS:

Jumping Crackers — perform their best antics on hard ground or paving.

Pin Wheels — Use a strong pin fixed firmly to a post. Fix the pin to slope very slightly downwards from the post. This keeps the wheel near the head of the pin and prevents it binding against the post.

Pom-Pom Cannons — The warning spurt of sparks is for 5 seconds before the bang.

Flyers or Flying Imps — Stand clear when you have lit the touchpaper as they fly in any direction.

Roman Candles & Long Fountains — Fix them firmly in an upright position by pushing them into soft earth.

Volcanos, Mount Vesuvius and Short Fountains — Stand them on a level surface before lighing.

Air Bombs and Star Shells — Fix them firmly in an upright position, clear of buildings and overhead constructions.

Wear an old glove for those marked "To be held in the hand." Never get over the top of a firework to light it (or after you have lit it). Light it at arms length.

He approached a large wooden pushcart that was selling these explosive devices on his walk along the river.

"What's with all the pyrotechnics?" he asked the old man manning the cart, pointing to a large rocket in the man's hand. "What's going on? Some holiday, or something?"

"A Yank, ain'tcha?" laughed the man, showing a missing row of front teeth. "I can always tell," and he continued to chuckle. "You guys have your own celebration over there, I know, from when you decided to go it alone. Independence Day ya calls it. Ha! You'll be back. Time will tell. With your tails between your legs, just you wait!" The old man started coughing he was laughing so hard."

Billy just stared at him, placing his hands on his hips.

"Nah, nah, nah, just yankin' your chain, champ," said the toothless wonder. "Don't be throwing me to the river there. I'll enlighten you, mate. Tis comin' soon enough."

And the old man explained to Billy the reason for the fireworks, stopping from time to time to ring up a sale.

"Comin' fast, it is. The fifth of November, lad. That's Bonfire Night. Some folks calls it Guy Fawkes Night, they do. That scoundrel, Fawkes, was part of what was called the Gunpowder Plot. That was way back in 1605, mind ya."

The man paused to light up his own cigarette. Billy lit another of his. Each man blowing out his smoke at the same time.

"Anyways," the old man continued, "they was planning to blow up the House of Lords with good old King James the First along with it as well. To cut to the chase as they say, Fawkes was caught. The plot was foiled, it was. Everyone was so excited that the king had survived that they lit bonfires all around London. We've been observing that glorious night ever since. It's a wonder the whole bloody town hasn't burnt to the ground, I tell ya. Can't tell the smoke from the fog most times. Folks have been collectin' firewood for weeks by now. The man in the moon could probably see London on Bonfire Night, for sure."

And he laughed himself into another coughing fit, spitting into a ragged handkerchief and putting it back into his pocket.

"Thanks for the history lesson, my friend," Billy said as he started walking away. He was about to shake the man's hand but thought better of it.

"You might want to buy wads of cotton for your ears, mate," called the old man. "Thank the good lord above I'm nearly deaf and can't hear most of the bloody things anyway."

"If you're mostly deaf," laughed Billy, "how could you hear what I was saying?"

"What?" the old man replied with a wink.

Billy continued on his long walk around the beautiful city, crossing back over the Thames by way of the Waterloo Bridge. Again, he stopped midway across the bridge to light up another Lucky Strike and to watch some boats glide slowly underneath.

When he noticed that it was probably time between performances, he headed to that pub not far from the theater. He had told Veronica his plans earlier and she would take a peek inside the pub to see if he had made it back in time. If not, they would meet again later that night back at the flat.

As he was approaching Covent Garden a group of five or six children of various ages were pushing an old wooden wheelbarrow down the street toward him. In the wheelbarrow was propped up what looked like a dummy, the clothes were stuffed with straw and a big floppy hat was placed on its head. One of the little kids ran up to Billy, hand outstretched.

"Penny for the guy?" the urchin asked.

Billy had no idea what that meant. He shrugged his shoulders and shook his head no. The boy then scampered ahead, asking another pedestrian the same thing, no doubt. Billy noticed that the person gave the boy some coins.

The pub was bustling. The matinee performance had ended and thirsty theater patrons were looking for a relaxing drink or five before heading home or to stay here to dine. Billy signaled to the barman, a different one than before, for a scotch, neat. He took his first sip and Veronica quietly sneaked up behind him, whispering lustily into his ear.

"Hey, handsome, want some company?"

Without reacting or turning around, Billy answered.

"If you're standing behind me, how do you know I'm handsome?"

Veronica laughed.

"Look up, cowboy. Look up," she said.

"Oh," he said as he looked up and saw his reflection in the mirror behind the bar. He hadn't even noticed that before.

"Besides," said Veronica, sidling up next to him, "if I was *really* a lady of the evening looking for my next trick, you could be Quasimodo and I'd *still* call you handsome. Don't let it go to your head."

Veronica ordered a Sloe Gin Fizz and asked Billy about his day.

"I'm assuming that nobody tried to shoot you, stab you, or seduce you in my absence while you were out and about," she joked.

"No, I'm safe on all counts. I had a great little history lesson though," he answered and then told her about the fireworks salesman.

"Oh, yes, the infamous Bonfire Night," Veronica said, shaking her head. "The night that's a living nightmare to every dog, cat, and horse in town, what with all those fireworks blasting from every street corner. To say nothing of those dangerous fires."

"Okay, something the man *didn't* tell me about though was what I saw a while ago not far from here."

He told her about the street kids and their dummy in the wheelbarrow.

"Ah, well," began Veronica, "that dummy is an effigy of Guy Fawkes. When they asked you 'Penny for the guy' they were really asking you for some loose change so they could afford to buy fireworks. You'll probably see several more of those effigies and wheelbarrows over the next few days. Those effigies are burned on the bonfires. Did that old man happen to tell you about Mischief Night as well?"

"No, that he didn't mention either. When's that?"

"That's the night *before* Bonfire Night. Almost like the night we have before Halloween back home in the States. Kids play all kinds of pranks, mostly harmless stuff like ringing doorbells and running away, or letting out the air from car tires. Silly, stupid stuff like that. Sometimes they've been known to steal really good firewood from rival bonfires. It's best if we stay inside. Well, I guess I will be. Inside and onstage."

"You're right, that does sound like Halloween back home," Billy said. "Some people called that Mischief Night too, but in the part of New Jersey where I'm from we called it Cabbage Night. It was reserved for just the teenagers, though.

He chuckled to himself.

"Hehehe...I remember one time Peyton and I...oh, never mind," and he stopped himself from going further.

"What?" asked Veronica.

"Nope. Someday when I'm drunk enough I might tell you. Let's just say that it has something to do with a pressed ham and leave it at that for the time being."

He continued chuckling to himself as Veronica simply shook her head.

26

Gregory Montgomery and Mildred Winsom angrily, nervously paced back and forth in one of the two rooms they had checked into at a tiny off-the-beaten-path guesthouse an hour's drive from London. It was, in their words, a rat hole in Ratfyn, but no one would ever think to look for the great actor here. Being that Devon Stone had returned home from Serbia unharmed, Mildred had vacated her house once again.

"I don't like the way things are going," Mildred said, with anger in her eyes. "I thought we had just about everything taken care of. Done and gone with. Something or somebody must have stirred the pot and gotten things going in the wrong direction. Wrong for *us*, that is!"

"I don't like that guy who's been hanging around Veronica all the time. Aside from what else we hoped to get done, I was hoping for a better relationship with her, if you know what I mean," whimpered Gregory.

"Oh, please, you're not fooling anyone with your act," sneered Mildred. "Does Christopher know? Wait. What guy? Who do you mean?"

"That American guy. He's been popping into her dressing room all the time now. Reeking of his stinking cigarette smoke and loving her up and down. Makes me sick."

"When did *he* come on the scene?"

"Oh, he popped over a few weeks ago, I think. She's been doing nothing but mooning over him when he shows up. He's staying at her place, too. Scandalous, I tell you!"

"Grow up, Gregory. Ye gods, you make me want to puke."

Gregory sat down on the side of his bed with a plop. He folded his arms and pouted. Mildred mulled over the things that Gregory had just said.

"How long has this been going on? I mean, how long have they known each other?" Mildred asked.

"It's been going on for a while. Long distance, I suppose. They met when she was in the USO shows and he was in the service," answered Gregory.

"Really, now. Hmmm. And you said he smoked. Happen to know what brand?"

"Oh, yes, he touts them like he's a stock holder or something. Lucky Strike. That's not a popular brand over here. Why do you ask?"

"Hmmmmm," said Mildred once again. "What were the chances? What a lucky strike indeed. Looks like we might need to add a couple more names to our list."

Billy was up and out bright and early the next morning. He was as excited about Mischief Night and Bonfire Night as a teenaged boy. He hastily made his way back to the walk along the Thames in hopes that the old man with the fireworks was still there. He was. Today a grizzled old dog kept him company. The dog was lying on its side, in the shade of the large pushcart, paying no attention to the people passing by.

"Remember me?" asked Billy, "The good ol' U.S. of A. might not be coming back to England, old guy, but *I'm* coming back to give you some good ol' business."

"Are ya, now, lad? Gonna set the town ablaze are ya?" and he snickered until it started a coughing fit.

"I see you brought some company with you today," Billy said, acknowledging the sleeping dog.

"Aye. Jamie's a good old boy, he is. Keeps better company than me wife, he does. No complaining. No smart backtalk."

Billy kneeled down to pet the dog. As soon as he felt Billy's hand gently stroke his back, the dog slowly opened his eyes and his tail began to wag, flopping quietly on the sidewalk.

"So, what is it that you want today, lad? Want enough noise to wake the dead, do ya?"

Billy laughed as he stood up, the dog lifting his head to keep looking at him.

"I haven't played around with this kind of stuff since I was a kid. Those Jumping Crackers look interesting. I'll have a couple dozen of those. Throw in a couple of those Roman Candles while you're at it."

"Ya bring a sack with ya to carry your arsenal here, bucko?" asked the toothless wonder.

"No."

"Ya got deep pockets?"

"No."

"Jaysus, what good are ya, then?" laughed the man. He found a big, wrinkled old paper bag under his cart and shook it open. He started ringing up Billy's purchases.

"Throw a couple more of those Jumping Crackers in there, will you, please?" said Billy. "I don't know what those Flying Imps do, but they look interesting. I'll try one or two."

"Half a crown more, lad, and ya can have the whole damn cart here. Jaysus!"

Billy paid the man, tipping his hat, as the dog got up, stretched, shook from muzzle to tail, and sniffed Billy in a rather rude manner.

Half an hour later Billy was a few blocks from the flat. He saw a small group of young boys pushing a wheelbarrow with a dummy sitting in it flopped haphazardly to one side. The smallest boy ran up to Billy with his hand outstretched.

"A penny for the guy?" he asked.

Billy reached into his pocket, pulling out a couple coins. Then he reached into the bag of his recent purchases and pulled out six Jumping Crackers and a Roman candle. He handed the lot to the little boy, whose eyes grew wide. He took this new treasure and scampered back to the rest of his little friends. They all turned to Billy, waving and smiling. Billy continued on his way. *Cute little urchins*, he thought.

Stooping down to pick up a shilling that was lying on the sidewalk, Billy laughed out loud a few minutes later when he heard a couple of the firecrackers go off somewhere behind him.

"Oh my *god*, have you been hit? Are you all right, sir?" yelled a well-dressed businessman excitedly as he ran up to Billy. "My heart stopped when I saw that!"

"Excuse me?" answered a confused Billy as he stood up again, turning around to see if perhaps the man was speaking to someone behind him.

"That car that just came tearing down the street. Didn't you see it? I was certain I saw someone taking a shot at you from it as it passed."

"I heard the firecrackers," said Billy, shrugging his shoulders. "I wasn't paying any attention to the traffic on the street. It was just firecrackers, wasn't it?"

"Not sure about firecrackers, young man. Whoever was in that car is a piss-poor shot, that's all I can say. I was sure I had seen a gun in that woman's hand. I don't know who you are, but you'd better be careful, sir. I have a feeling you're on someone's list. We're not accustomed to random shootings around here. Calling a Bobby won't help. I can barely describe the car and I certainly didn't get a license number, it all happened so fast. I thought you had been hit when I saw you drop to the ground. My nerves are shattered for the day. I can only imagine yours."

Billy stood there in confusion, still not grasping what the man was saying. The sidewalk was slowly filling with other pedestrians; seemingly unaware of anything dangerous that may or may not have just transpired. The businessman picked up his attaché case from the sidewalk where he had dropped it a few minutes earlier.

"This is what I bent down for," Billy said, extending his hand, showing the man the coin.

"Save it, by all means, as your lucky charm, then, sir. It may have saved your life. But please, watch your back, my good man, that's all I can say for now," he said as he started on his way again.

"Thanks. I guess," Billy called out to him, still confused.

He continued walking, occasionally looking up and down the street.

He turned the corner leading to Veronica's apartment building. Coming toward him on the sidewalk was a very garishly dressed redheaded woman of indeterminate age wearing far too much makeup. As they approached each other the woman smiled at him, giving him an extravagant wink and running her tongue salaciously back and forth along her top ruby-red lip. Her perfume was overwhelming.

Billy tipped his hat to her and continued on his way, a bit quicker pace to his step.

"Well, good morning, bright eyes," Veronica called from the kitchen when she heard Billy enter the flat. "Obviously you were on a mission. What's going on?"

"All I can say," Billy answered, coming into the kitchen and placing the bag with his purchases on the table, "is that assassins and hookers start awfully early around here!"

———————————

Mildred Winsom had cursed out loud when her shot went astray. She always had trouble navigating the busy streets of London and drove in the city rarely, avoiding it as much as she could. Hitting an unseen pothole at an inappropriate moment made her furious. Driving one-handed and trying to aim at a walking target on a sidewalk was a stunt that just didn't work out in her favor this morning. Her bullet *did* manage to shatter a large pot filled with dead, dried geraniums that had been sitting on a table in someone's garden, however, causing no further harm.

27

Veronica stood, hands placed firmly on her hips, staring at him.

"Hookers I can understand. What did you mean by 'assassins', Billy?"

He poured himself a cup of coffee and grabbed a banana from a bowl on the counter. He explained what had happened on his walk back from the Thames and the firecracker salesman. Veronica stared at him and then cleared her throat before she spoke.

"The hooker's name is Delores. Not sure if that's her real name or not. Doesn't matter. She's been working this neighborhood for years. Must do a fair amount of business being that she claims this as her territory. She's even come to see my show, believe it or not. We've chatted a few times. God help Peyton if she ever spies *him*!"

Billy bit into his banana, arching an eyebrow.

"Now, regarding that *other* word you mentioned when you first came in here this morning."

•

Mildred Winsom was getting frustrated with the way the situation had escalated. She and her group had been convinced that there were only three more names that had to be eliminated before they would be in the clear. Now a few more people seem to have been drawn into the events. She was *not* happy about it at all!

She made a hasty decision and called each one of her remaining team.

•

"Honestly, Billy," Veronica started her lecture, "I think it's time you moved out."

"Are you saying you don't want me staying here in the apartment anymore?" he responded with a frown.

"That's *not* what I mean at all. And I think you know that. You simply need to pack up and go back home. Somebody is after you here…maybe me, too, for that matter, but it's not *our* battle. We got involved by accident and then we compounded the situation by trying to play detective. It's not funny anymore. Not that it ever was! We're not Nick and Nora Charles, and definitely not Sherlock and Watson. You certainly know I don't like this murderous cat and mouse game that Devon Stone and his remaining group is playing. Not. At. All."

"I have no intention of arguing about this with you, Ronnie. I agree, in part, with what you're saying. It's obviously gotten dangerous for us and, yes, that was beyond our control. But I am *not* leaving. I don't know how much protection I can be, considering that I now seem to be someone's target, but I'll do my best to keep *you* from harm."

"Well what about your obligation to Peyton and to your business back home? You've been here for weeks, now."

"Peyton is a big boy. He knows the situation and can handle the store back home. He has a cousin that has helped out with the store before. I'm sure he's using her if it gets too hectic."

Veronica was silent, pacing back and forth, fighting tears.

"I'll accompany you to the theater every night. I'll stay backstage, out of everyone's way, I promise. But at least I'll feel as though I'm offering *some* form of protection. Maybe."

Veronica stopped pacing. She sat down abruptly on the sofa and let the tears flow.

•

It was at that instant, watching Veronica cry, that Billy pulled the reality of the situation into sharper focus. The operative word was *reality*. Billy's world of reality was a harsh one, or had been. His world had been one of war. He played an active part in it. He had been shot at. He had *been* shot. He had bombed and killed people. Sometimes *with* remorse, more often than not *without*. This current maelstrom had escalated into something increasingly dangerous, befuddling, and, to his chagrin, exhilarating. He was still battling an old enemy.

Veronica's world, on the other hand, dealt with illusion. One in which she plays a fictitious character within an imaginary setting upon a stage. A few laughs, a few tears, perhaps a song and dance or two, and everyone ends happily ever after. The curtain comes down. Tomorrow night at 8:40 it starts all over again. Same show, different audience. In *her* world, the word *bomb* takes on a whole different meaning.

Suddenly, and through no doings of their own, their two worlds were colliding.

Billy sat down next to Veronica, wrapping strong arms around her shoulders and pulling her in closer to him. She rested her head up against his, and sniffled. He was hoping that he could provide a happily ever after before the curtain came down.

28

Being the generous soul that he was and because he found them all so cute, Billy had given away all the firecrackers that he had bought. He couldn't resist the little kids begging "Penny for a guy" practically on every street now. So, once again he headed back to the Thames to try to find that irascible old man selling the fun, noisy explosive devices.

He saw the same old wooden pushcart ahead of him but there was a different, much younger person manning it. The same old dog was laying under the cart, sniffing the air and wagging his tail at all the passersby.

"Oh, you're new," said Billy as he came up to the cart.

"How did you know that?" abruptly asked the scruffy-looking man. He had the same basic look as the older guy who had sold the fireworks to Billy previously, but he was at least twenty years younger. A short stub of a burning cigarette was sticking out of the side of his mouth.

"How did I know *what?*" asked Billy, thinking that the young man was being sarcastic or simply being a belligerent smart aleck. "That you're new?"

"No," answered the kid. "Well, yes. How did you know me name? I ain't never seen ya b'fore. Do you know me, mate?"

Billy stared at him in confusion and shook his head like a rattle. The kid flicked his cigarette out toward the river, missing it by at least five feet.

"Maybe I missed something right at the start," said Billy. "I have a feeling one of us is confused. I didn't mention your name. What is it?"

"Yes, you did, mate. New," answered the young man, now with a sly grin on his face. "I ain't kiddin' ya. It's New. I'm Joe New."

Billy looked at him, rolled his eyes and shook his head.

"Okay, now I get it," Billy said with a bit of a laugh. "Have you taken over this spot? Where's the other guy?"

"That's me old man, Ralphie New," answered Joe New. "He went out on a hellova bender last night and is still out stone cold so I'm filling in. Today I'm the new New. He's the old New."

"Who knew?" asked Billy, now laughing hysterically. "Right, and who knew that this exchange would turn into an Abbott and Costello routine?"

"Who?" asked Joe New.

"He's on first," laughed Billy even harder.

Now Joe New looked confused.

After Billy retained his composure, he bought three-dozen more of the Jumping Crackers and six of the Pom-Pom Cannons. He had brought the old paper sack that the old New had given him on his very first purchase. He thanked the new New for the laugh, paid for his firecrackers and bent down to pet Jamie, the old dog. The New dog.

He headed back toward Veronica's flat, keeping a mindful eye on passing traffic and hoping to avoid Delores should she be making her rounds.

29

Earlier in the day, Police Inspector Vanderhoff had called Devon Stone with an embarrassing request.

"I'm so sorry to bother you with this drivel, Mr. Stone, but my wife has been quite persistent. Ever since I've begun this investigation she's been hounding me to meet you. As I mentioned to you weeks ago, she has read all of your books, sometimes even twice, including the newest one. I don't know what plans you might have today, sir, but could she possibly stop by your place for a quick chat and to have you autograph one of your books?"

Devon sighed, rolled his eyes but let his ego answer for him.

"Well, I'd be extremely flattered, Inspector. Have her stop around at three-ish, could you?"

"I, for one, will be eternally grateful, Mr. Stone. Her demands have been relentless. I'll be able to sleep better. You are, indeed, a true gentleman."

His front doorbell chimed and Devon glanced at his watch. Precisely 3:21. *She's late*, he thought, *but I* did *say 3-ish*.

He opened the door to reveal a plumpish woman, perhaps in her late fifties, wearing a black overcoat and a flashy red hat with exotic bird feathers sticking out in one direction. She was wearing bright red gloves to match the garish hat. Her smiling face had perhaps a dab too much rouge on her cheeks and her perfume was so overpowering that Devon feared he might sneeze. She clutched a small handbag and was holding Devon's latest bestseller in her hand. Her taxicab slowly pulled away from the curb behind her.

"Oh, good afternoon, Mr. Stone," she gushed with a singsong voice. "I am *so* thrilled to be here, never thinking that I'd *ever* get the chance to actually meet you. You have no idea. I believe my dear husband called earlier. I'm Edna Vanderhoff. May I come in?"

Devon opened the door wider to allow her entrance. As she stepped forward, she dropped the book and withdrew a small caliber pistol from her purse.

Devon's memory immediately kicked into overdrive. Standing before him was the woman he had seen with the two frisky lovers, the late Jacob Everett and the still-missing Mildred Winsom, at the Rose Bush pub back on June 16th, at 9:22 P.M.

They moved further into the foyer, Mrs. Vanderhoff pushing the front door closed with her foot.

"My, my," said Devon with the start of a wry smile on his face. "What an eye-opening surprise."

"Mr. Stone, relish that surprise for a brief moment. You won't have long to enjoy it."

"So, *you* must be the evasive missing link that we've been seeking. Is your husband aware of your murderous doings, or is he a participant we never even suspected?"

"Oh, no, he is completely oblivious to my doings outside of our modest home. As long as a hot meal is waiting for the poor sap when he gets home, he's content. He's ignored me for years, old limp-dick that he is. He couldn't solve a crime if he witnessed it whilst it was happening. I keep my politics contained within. He has *no* idea that I wish Hitler had succeeded with his plans to get rid of all those filthy kikes. My friends and I have been trying to right the injustices served up by those Night Witches. Night *bitches*! We have a feeling that you and your raggedy little band, albeit diminished in numbers, are getting *way* to close for comfort. It's time *you* were dealt with. We were going to save *you* for the grand finale, so to speak. As the grand prize for which ever one of us did you in. We wanted you to see your little group get killed off one by one. But I'm taking it upon myself to do the nasty deed. Aren't *I* the lucky one? Pity, too. I so thoroughly enjoyed your books, Mr. Stone. Ironic, isn't it? Your last book, *The Fallen*, and now *you* will be one of the fallen."

"I take it, then, that you plan to shoot me, walk calmly out of here and simply head back home to your hot kitchen and clueless husband as though nothing has happened here, right?"

"Oh, come now, Mr. Stone. I thought better of you than that. I'm surprised. Tsk, tsk. No, no. I'm not going to shoot *you*. *You* are going to shoot *me*."

•

Veronica was rushing around, trying to get ready to head out to the theater for this evening's performance. Billy was gallivanting around the city trying to see what the mischievous children of London were doing on this holiday eve, keeping a mindful eye on slowly passing cars and avoiding dark alleys. Stepping from the tub, toweling dry, Veronica then wrapped her long robe around herself, as she was about to get dressed. There came a frantic knocking on the door to her flat. She frowned, running toward it, thinking that perhaps Billy had gotten into some sort of trouble or forgotten his key.

She opened the door and was pushed back so suddenly that she nearly lost her balance. Gregory Montgomery headed straight for her, wielding a small pistol and leaving the door wide open. She gasped.

"Gregory, what in the world? Where have you been? I've been so worried about you!"

"Stop the play-acting Veronica. I don't know how you got tangled up in all this mess but I'm sick of it. I never thought it would come down to this, but I'm putting an end to your involvement, no matter how minor it might be. I can't take the chance any longer."

"Gregory, I have no idea what you're talking about," Veronica lied, "but please calm down. Maybe you're just over stressed. Or something."

"It ends, Veronica. One by one. Your friend, Stone, is being taken care, probably at this very moment. At least he'll be out of the picture and soon you will be. And your boyfriend, too! I'm sorry, Veronica," he said as he raised the gun.

Veronica could feel her heart racing.

"Oh, thank God you've come back!" she said, looking as though she had seen someone behind Montgomery.

"Oh, good grief, Veronica, you're a much better actress than that. You expect me to fall for that old ploy that's been used in every god-awful B-movie since Hitchcock was in diapers?"

No sooner had he uttered those words than the blunt end of a pistol struck the back of his head, and he slumped to the floor.

"You're welcome!" said a smiling Peyton Chase, dropping his duffle bag to the floor.

Veronica glanced at him, then down to Gregory, and the pistol now lying next to him. She fainted.

Before she could hit the floor, Peyton rushed to catch her. He carried her gently into her bedroom, laying her carefully on her bed. When he returned to the living room a few minutes later, Gregory Montgomery and his pistol had vanished.

•

Devon Stone knew *exactly* what Edna Vanderhoff meant to do. He had used this situation in his latest book, *The Fallen*, a novel about revenge killing. The bad guy, wearing gloves, bludgeoned one of the good guys. Then the bad guy gave himself a superficial wound, putting the pistol in the good guy's now dead hand to get the poor man's fingerprints on the trigger. Then, claiming self-defense was able to get away scot-free... only to be caught, however, later in the book. Devon was hoping for a better outcome, at the moment, than that poor, framed man in his book. But how?

"I know the floor plan for houses like this one, Mr. Stone. I know that there is a basement door just behind these stairs. It's a pity that you'll suffer a horrible fall, breaking your handsome neck, as I fight you off defending my dignity. The press will have a field day considering your notoriety. A famed author, trying to molest a poor old lady. And shooting her in the leg because she resisted your charms, no less!"

Keeping her distance, she backed him down the hallway and reached for the door to the basement. Keeping an eye on her target, she reached to open the door. When she did so, she was confused by the strange glow that was coming from down below. She was even more confused, and then alarmed, by the man that was about to reach the very top step. He was carrying a small basket. It was the cantankerous elderly man from next door with the unruly grey hair.

Her momentary shock and loss of attention was all the time that Devon Stone needed. He rushed her, knocking the pistol from her hand, sending it sliding down the shiny hardwood flooring in the hallway. Grabbing her from behind, pulling her head back with his left hand and quickly placing his right arm around the plump woman's neck, he squeezed in, under her chin, as hard as he could, performing a classic jujitsu move, shime-waza, a chokehold in other words, across her windpipe. Stronger than he had expected considering her apparent age, she struggled, trying to kick out from behind almost causing him to lose balance but he maintained his stance, squeezing harder and harder. She tried desperately to call out but it was impossible. Just garbled sounds came from the woman's mouth. Effectively cutting off her air supply to her brain, she weakened as he continued to apply pressure. She tried to grab at his arms to pull him away but her heavy overcoat seemed to restrict her attempts.

"What a shame, Edna," he whispered into her ear as he tightened the pressure even more. "I fear that poor Inspector Limp Dick will be going hungry this evening."

Her struggling ceased. A matter of moments and she slumped to the floor, no longer breathing and Devon no longer wanting to hold up the bulky woman.

"Chester," he said calmly, indicating the motionless lump on his hardwoods, "allow me to introduce you to Mrs. Edna Vanderhoff. The heretofore unknown and mysterious number three."

And then there were two.

•

At precisely 6:17 Devon Stone placed a phone call and was lucky enough to reach Inspector Vanderhoff still at the police station.

"Inspector," said Stone with a slight note of alarm in his voice. "So glad that I was able to reach you. I sincerely hope that your wife is all right. Do you know if her plans had changed for any reason? I've been waiting here at home for hours and she never showed up."

"Oh, dear," said the inspector. "Oh, dear."

30

"So, what's the situation back home?" asked Billy, "I mean with your family situation."

The two men were having a couple beers while waiting for Veronica, as she got ready to head out to the theater. Even after the unsettling excitement with Gregory Montgomery, she was ready to perform. A true professional. Veronica had been deeply touched by the story regarding the beloved actress Beatrice Lillie during World War II. Just before she went on stage one evening, she was informed of her only son's death in action. She refused to postpone her performance. "I'll cry tomorrow," she had said. Her audience that night never knew the heartbreak that the performer was enduring.

"It was extremely emotional," answered Peyton, "as you can imagine, for a few days after I got back home. My dad crumbled like a cake. He and Mom had been married, like, forever. They met in kindergarten, for chrissakes!"

Billy had known Peyton's parents all his life and was well aware of the strong love within that family.

"Honestly," continued Peyton, "I doubt if they had ever spent a night apart. Ever! Even when I was born Dad slept in the hospital next to Mom. But he's more resilient than I had originally thought. A few days of tears… and I mean a *lot* of tears…from both me and him, and he pulled himself together."

"What's next for him?" asked Billy.

"Well, that's the odd part. The part that took me sort of by surprise. Needless to say, I told him about what was going on over here. He's the one who encouraged me to get my ass back here to help in any way I could."

"He *encouraged* you to get back in harm's way?" asked an incredulous Billy.

"Damn right!" exclaimed Peyton. "He was enthralled when I told him about the Night Witches. Of course, I had to tell him about that hot chick Anoushka."

Billy just shook his head and laughed.

"Well then, what about the gun shop?" asked Billy.

"My dad volunteered to take over. My mom had been ill for a long time and he didn't want to leave her side. Now that she's gone, he has a new purpose. Believe it or not, Billy, he knows guns just about as much as you and me. He and my cousin Karen will be handling the store until we get back. *If* we get back."

"You can eighty-six those last four words, Peyton. We *will* be back!" barked Billy. "But, wait. Your dad *and* Karen? Together? Your dad is so easy going, mild mannered and…"

"Yeah, yeah, I know," interrupted Peyton, shrugging his shoulders. "And Karen is a loud, abrasive, snippy, short-tempered, opinionated, argumentative, sarcastic bitch. What could possibly go wrong? I'd like to be a fly on the wall their first day together in the shop. Even poor old Buster goes into hiding when Karen is around."

Buster, named after Buster Keaton, was his dad's Irish Setter.

"Okay, but *now* we have *this* situation going on here," said Billy, turning their attention back to Veronica's attacker and accomplices. "Your dad didn't want to leave your mom's side and I don't really want to leave Veronica's. Now that you're back, buddy, we can work this thing together. Go back into your bedroom and get your clothes off. We're going to the theater."

31

Fearful that the recent activity towards them was getting a bit more dicey, Billy and Peyton accompanied Veronica to the theater. When the doors opened, and with their two house seat tickets in hand, they were shown to their seats in the audience, keeping a mindful eye to those in the audience who might look suspicious. Members of the audience, however, cast some reproachful stares at the two American men.

London theatergoers were advised to wear evening attire while attending performances in the West End. Billy had packed a suit and two sports jackets for this recent stay. Peyton had none of that. Wearing one of Billy's sports jackets and one of his dress shirts, the eyebrows of several elegantly attired theatre-goers were raised by his dungarees. The jacket and shirt were tight as it was, with Peyton's more muscular frame, but there was no way he'd fit into any of Billy's trousers. Neither man had shiny black shoes, either. Billy tried to ignore the rude stares and chatted nonchalantly with Peyton before the performance began. Peyton slunk as low as he could go in his seat without actually sliding off onto the floor. Billy had worn his very best suit on the night of his arrival weeks before, when he watched the play for the first time. If he had been the recipient of any chastising stares he had been oblivious to them. Tonight, however, with his friend in tow, was another matter.

An appropriately dressed couple entered the aisle on Peyton's side and the lady non-too-subtly switched seats with her husband when she realized she'd be sitting next to Peyton.

The lights hadn't dimmed yet but there was a smattering of applause, starting at the back of the theater working its way toward the stage. People turned their heads to look and few even stood up. Billy and Peyton looked at each other and shrugged their shoulders. A man, *not* in evening attire, but a rumpled suit, was being shown to his seat, third row center. He acknowledged the audience nodding his head from side to side and a little wave of his hand.

Billy turned to the woman on his side. She was beaming and applauding quietly.

"Is that someone I should know?" he asked.

She gave him a smile that really wasn't the friendliest of smiles he had ever seen.

"He's the playwright of what we are about to see, young man. That's Noel Coward himself."

Veronica told Billy and Peyton after the show that Coward had just come from a late afternoon full dress rehearsal for his latest play, *Quadrille*, starring Alfred Lunt and Lynn Fontanne. Neither men knew either of the two performers she mentioned, but guessed that it must be some big deal. What really *was* a big deal was that Noel Coward had visited Veronica backstage following the performance and told her that he was so impressed that he wanted to write a play specifically for her. Perhaps a musical.

She was on cloud nine and would sleep very well that night with nary a thought about assassins.

•

Waiting at the stage door, amid a throng of adoring fans, Mildred Winsom stood back in silence as she stared at the exiting actors and actresses. Veronica Barron and the boyfriend she had recently found out about. One opportunity had already been thwarted, to her chagrin, because of a pothole. Now, evidently, a *third* person had to be dealt with. A typical American in inappropriate and poorly fitting attire.

She reached into her oversized handbag and pulled out her newly purchased Land Camera. As if she was an adoring fan, she pointed the camera at the smiling trio now standing at the door and clicked the shutter. *They*, of course, had no idea what Mildred Winsom looked like. A minute later she was holding in her hand a small black and white Polaroid photograph of her next targets.

32

Sunday morning, no performances today and Veronica and Billy expected to sleep late. As late as possible. Maybe all day, with the covers pulled up over their heads. Too many emotions running through their respective minds over the past few weeks. Veronica let out a loud groan as her telephone rang at 8:35.

"Good morning, Veronica," said a chipper-sounding Devon Stone as she answered. "And it *is* certainly a good morning. I hope I haven't called too early."

Veronica yawned and Billy rolled over in bed frowning at whoever would be calling this early.

"And good morning right back to you, Devon," said Veronica, causing Billy to roll his eyes and sink his head, face first, deep into his pillow.

"Look," continued Devon Stone, "I know you two have gone through a lot these past few weeks. I guess your friend, Peyton, has as well. I thought you might like to get out of the city for the day and try to get your minds off the horrible situation at hand."

"Frankly, Devon," Veronica said, trying to conceal her annoyance, "I'd like to crawl under my bed and hide there until after the coronation next year."

Devon laughed.

"Completely understand, my dear, completely. Anyway, I've got to run out to the coast along the Channel for a bit of research for my next book.

Believe it or not, even with all this nonsense going on regarding the chasing of assassins, I actually have work to do. I want to make sure all the details about the Dover Castle and the lighthouse out there are accurate. Can't have any bloody nitpickers tearing my facts apart, you know."

Veronica tried to wrap her head around what Devon was saying. He's being cool as a cucumber. He's being pursued by who knows how many more assassins. He and his associates have murdered an unknown number (to her) of those so-called assassins this past year. And now he's worried about getting the details just right for his next book? *Am I in the middle of a nightmare directed by Alfred Hitchcock?* she thought to herself.

"Well, I suppose that would be a nice change," answered Veronica with a slight shrug to her shoulders. "Let me ask Billy. We really didn't have any specific plans for today, you know, aside from hiding from anyone or anything that moves outdoors."

"Peyton is more than welcome to accompany us as well. I'll see if Anoushka is free today," said Devon as he glanced at his watch. "It's, at most, a two-hour drive the way I drive and I'll even supply a nice picnic lunch."

Devon Stone had checked a certain timetable and wanted to reach the cliffs at high tide.

"All right, then, Devon," Veronica said as she came back on the line. "Billy is in agreement. We haven't heard Peyton stirring yet in his room but I'm sure he'll be glad to get away from this nonsense, at least for a few hours."

"Splendid!" Devon responded. "I shall pick you all up in front of your building in one hour. Will that give everyone time enough?"

One hour on the dot later, Devon Stone pulled his shiny Armstrong Siddeley Sapphire alongside the curb in front of Veronica's building, and hopped out, leaving the engine running. The three Americans had been waiting on the steps and approached the sleek car. Both Billy and Peyton stopped in their tracks when they got closer to the vehicle. They both let out a low whistle.

"Is that a car or is that a *car*!" exclaimed Billy, clearly impressed with what he was seeing.

Both of the men walked all around the car, leaning closer to inspect one feature after the other. The car, so sparkling clean that it appeared to be still wet, was a deep Hunter Green, with buff-colored genuine leather seats. Peyton leaned especially close to look at the shiny chrome hood ornament sitting atop the chrome V-shaped radiator grille.

"Is that a...?" he began.

"Yes, it is" Devon answered the unfinished question. "That's a Sphinx. The symbol of silence."

How fitting. There was stunned silence from the trio.

"Hop in, kids, let's get going," said Devon as he opened the rear door. "There's plenty of leg room for you three back there. We'll be picking up Anoushka on the way and she can ride up front with me."

With Veronica sitting between them, Billy and Peyton were both hoping for a chance to drive this car sometime today. Unless, of course, some crazed assassin would be waiting for them at the White Cliffs of Dover. But then, they were clearly aware of the sophisticated, albeit cold-blooded assassin who was driving this spectacular car.

•

Anoushka had been staying with a friend of hers from Russia who had been visiting England. She was staying at a little guesthouse in Canterbury. Devon pulled his car into the car park but didn't have to leave the vehicle. Anoushka came running out to greet him, waving goodbye to her beautiful friend.

Peyton leaned across Veronica to speak to Billy.

"If all the chicks in Russia look like those two," he said with a wink, "I'm heading there after all this is over."

"Oh, grow up," snickered Veronica.

"Off we go again," said Devon glancing at his watch. "We should be there in twenty-three minutes, tops."

Twenty-two minutes later Devon slowed his car and turned into a nice, remote parking area, a short distance from the sheer drop-off of the famous cliffs. There were no other cars around. They would have the place all to themselves. The brilliant sun shone overhead in a cloudless sky. They all inhaled the smell of the surf crashing below. Sea gulls swooped up and around the area, carried by the stiff breeze blowing along the Channel. Their calls were the only music the group needed to create a pleasant, relaxing atmosphere.

"If I remember correctly from the last time I was here, there is a very nice walking path along the edge up that way," as he pointed northward. "There should be a nice spot for our picnic luncheon. I assume you're all hungry about now, right?"

There were agreements all the way around.

"I shall get the basket from the boot," Devon said, as he walked around to the rear of the car. "Billy, here's a blanket you can spread if you'd like," he continued, as he tossed him a blanket that was covering the picnic basket. "Go on ahead. I'll be right with you. Mind the path, though. That's quite a drop if you lose your footing."

The three Americans and Anoushka found the hiking trail and headed away from the car. Their walking rustled up several little blue butterflies, which took flight as they walked past. Devon waited a few minutes, watching as they went, and reached back into the boot. Sticking out from under another blanket was the handle of a knife. He leaned in, taking hold of it, and checking his watch one more time. It was high tide.

33

Devon Stone removed the knife from beneath the blanket and walked to the edge of the cliffs, making sure, again, that he was not visible to his traveling companions.

"Freddy, Freddy, Freddy, you cheap bastard," Devon said to himself as he inspected his previous attacker's weapon. "I'm terribly disappointed that you didn't think my neck was worth more that this shoddy piece of garbage. I was hoping to use it myself on one of your cohorts for the sheer irony of it all, but this will *never* do."

He held the knife by the tip of the blade, raised his arm back and with a strong thrust he let out a loud grunt as he sent the knife spiraling through the air.

"Goodbye, Freddy," he whispered as he watched the knife fall toward the waves crashing against the cliffs below. The sun glistened on the blade until it sunk beneath the pounding surf.

Devon smiled to himself. Two months ago, very late at night, he had stood at this same spot tossing the body of the knife's owner, Fredrik Mooreland, down to the roiling waters below. Devon had played his attacker like a Steinway piano, luring him into, what Fredrik had thought, was a surprise attack outside of the pub. Freddy hadn't been the only target of Devon's to meet this same fate, at this same spot…at high tide.

Devon just wanted to keep his activities at this spot a secret from the others. Not that it really mattered.

•

Devon carried the picnic basket to the rest of the group who were already seated on the ground on top of the colorful blanket. He opened the basket with a dramatic flourish to reveal fine china, crystal wine glasses, silverware, various cold meats, fruits, and cheeses along with three large bottles of Cabernet Franc. Nestled amongst all that was a large loaf of bread with a crispy golden crust.

"Whoa," whistled Peyton followed by a laugh, "you murderers sure know how to entertain!"

Both Veronica and Billy shot him a glare that was piercing. Devon chuckled.

"Let's leave my sideline out of the conversation, young man," said Devon, shaking his finger playfully at Peyton. "Today is a day simply for fun and relaxation. If you want to discuss murders, I'd be only too happy to discuss any of my books with you."

"I apologize, Devon," laughed Peyton. "I didn't mean to be impertinent. But I'm from New Jersey and it just comes naturally."

Devon uncorked a bottle of wine and poured a glass for everyone.

"A toast to happy endings," Devon exclaimed, holding his glass aloft.

•

Thirty minutes later, the food and most of the wine gone, Billy and Veronica lay back on the blanket gazing up into the sky. Devon sat, his arms wrapped around his up drawn legs, watching as Peyton and Anoushka wandered off along the path. They appeared to be in deep conversation.

"Everything was just delicious, Devon," said Veronica, "but that bread was exceptional. I've never tasted anything like it. I don't normally comment on bread, for Pete's sake. Did that come from a bakery near you?"

"No, no," answered Devon. "That bread certainly *is* special, isn't it? I have a very good friend who, in his retirement, has taken up a new hobby. Baking. He has come up with some very unique recipes, to say the least. I shall pass your comments along to him."

"I'll be damned," Billy exclaimed with a bit of a chuckle, and pointing up to the heavens. "There are actually really and truly bluebirds over the White Cliffs of Dover!"

"Well, to be perfectly accurate, Billy," answered Devon, "those are not *really* bluebirds. The bluebirds that you know of back in the States are not native here. Have *never* been here. What you're seeing swooping up over us now are swallows, oh, and that one", he said pointing to one very swiftly moving bird, "is a house martin. They have a bluish sheen to them, for sure, but they are truly not bluebirds."

"Does Vera Lynn know that?" asked Veronica sarcastically.

"As long as people keep buying her records, I'm sure Miss Lynn couldn't give a flying hoot," Devon responded.

"Changing the subject entirely," began Veronica, almost afraid to say what she was about to say.

"You're allowed," nodded Devon with a smile.

"I'm not sure where I want to go with this but do you believe in God, Devon?"

"Oh, I believe in many gods, Miss Barron. Dionysus, especially. I simply do not pray to any of them. There are even the Keres, horrible goddesses who personify violent death. Perhaps *they* pray to *me*! Why do you ask?"

Veronica thought for a moment.

"I haven't read any of your books. Not yet, that is. But you seem to handle…well…you treat death in a matter-of-fact way from what I have observed over the past few weeks. Does writing your mysteries inure you to mayhem?"

"Believe it or not, Veronica, you're not the first person to ask that of me. Let me ask something of *you*. Does my demeanor frighten you?"

Veronica giggled, putting her hand up to her mouth.

"I don't know if it's the wine or what, Devon, but suddenly I feel giddy. A bit lightheaded. No, you don't frighten me. You perplex me. At first I was aghast at what you and your companions are doing. Peyton was right, of course, calling you a murderer. Let's be totally frank here. You're actually a cold-blooded murderer, at that."

"So much for today being for fun and relaxation," blurted Billy.

"That afternoon at your place when you told us about the Night Witches I was enthralled," Veronica continued. "What a great story. Those brave, brave women. But then, you told us the rest of the story and I was appalled. I think, for the briefest of moments, I actually hated you."

Devon inhaled deeply, seriously mulling his next words.

"I don't take offense at what you say, my dear, certainly not. It wasn't too very long ago that the only murders I ever committed were simply with the written word and an appropriate page-count. I've lost count of *those* murders. But I have certainly learned a good deal from all my research. My friend Agatha Christie, by the way, is a genuine, certified expert on poisons, having been read by pathologists as reference material for poisoning cases of their own. Did you know that? And, recently, even *I* have called upon her expertise…although she need not know how or why," he said with a little sly wink.

"Personally," he continued, "I believe that this cause our little group is pursuing at the moment is a noble one. Is it *legal*? Absolutely not…just noble. But it all comes down to one basic fact involving semantics and point-of-view. According to us, *we* are fighting an enemy. *They*, on the other hand, consider *us* the enemy. It's a secret battle."

"But…but now," said a suddenly concerned Veronica, "the three of *us* know your secret."

Devon Stone thought about that for a second, pursing his lips. And then he smiled.

"I believe it was your own, very wise Benjamin Franklin who once said *three may keep a secret, if two of them are dead."* Devon had said that with a smile and another sly wink.

"Oooh-kay, then," said Billy, with a bit of a stammer and trying to change the subject as rapidly as he could. "Well, then, what starts the ball rolling? Regarding your *writing*, I mean."

"Very nice segue, Billy," smiled Devon, "I'm impressed. A bit awkward, but nicely done, young man,"

Billy wasn't sure if that comment was complimentary or sarcastic. But he decided to continue his line of questioning.

"How do you come up with the plots for your books, Devon? A microscopic germ of an idea generates into full-blown nefarious doings, for sure. Do you chart them out in notes before you write, or what? Obviously your next book will be placed around here somewhere, what with the research you have in mind for this afternoon."

"Intriguing question, Billy, interesting," answered Devon. "Again, asked of me several times. It might seem odd, but I often start with my characters first. After I've created a cast of characters in my mind, I have somewhat of a basic premise to start things off. A misdemeanor of some sort. I usually write the conclusion very early on, and then get my characters into situations that will somehow get them to that smashing, surprising, twist ending. The characters who survive, that is," and he chuckled. "The characters speak to me as I write. Sometimes they dictate their own actions. Strange as it may seem, sometimes a character that I have first conceived as being a hero turns out to be the villain. Or vice versa."

And which are you? Veronica thought to herself.

"And how does *this* story end, Devon?" asked Peyton who, along with Anoushka, had returned to the blanket. "The story that we all are living at the moment. Will it have a happy ending?"

Devon Stone sighed, looking out toward the water. The coastline of

France was shimmering in the distance, across the Strait of Dover. It was crystal clear.

"I haven't the foggiest," he acknowledged. "I'm not writing *this* one."

They all looked at one another.

"Come, kids, let's gather our things. We have a castle and a lighthouse to hit yet this afternoon. Research, you know? My publisher has given me a deadline. No pun intended."

34

The picnic basket was stored in the boot once again, but the happy picnickers casually passed the third bottle of wine around in the car as they headed off a short distance to the enormous Dover Castle. Some historians claimed that it was the largest castle in England. Others, debating the issue, were defiant in their opinions that that title belonged to Windsor Castle. Dating back to the eleventh century, the imposing castle was going to be one of the settings for Devon's next book. He was intrigued by a series of unsolved murders that had taken place in and around the area during the 1920s. He had no intention of being able to solve the still-open cases, but he wanted to glean as much information as possible and elaborate upon them to the point of his next book becoming another bestseller.

Billy and Peyton were intrigued by the role the castle and its underground tunnels had played during the war in which they fought. The evacuation of British and French soldiers from Dunkirk had been planned and directed by Admiral Sir Bertram Ramsay from his headquarters within the tunnels.

Devon Stone knew all the facts and figures surrounding the history of the castle, especially the trying times during the war. With a newly purchased camera, Devon snapped photo after photo so he could accurately get all the details of the site just right when he wrote his book. As he and his companions walked in and around the vast area, he functioned as a very well informed tour guide.

"You're not going to test us on any of this when we get back in the car, are you, Devon?" joked Peyton.

"*Before* you get back in the car, lad. Before!" laughed Devon. "Take notes if you intend to get a ride back to London this evening."

Although there was the Roman Lighthouse as part of the Dover Castle, another lighthouse, the South Foreland, a few miles to the northeast intrigued Devon as well. He planned to use both of them as locales for his fictitious grisly murders. They drove to it, and then walked around the grounds as Devon filled them in on historical facts and figures. His guests appeared to be listening intently, but he knew that anything he told them would be retained for no longer than two minutes. It didn't bother him. He had become accustomed to this throughout his life. He had no idea how this memory of his retained so much, but it had made him rich and famous.

It was a very productive day for the author, as well as a very enjoyable one. He was totally satisfied by this little outing. By the time they were all heading back on the road to London, with three of his passengers already dozing off in the back seat, Devon had created the complete cast of characters in his head, started formulating the reasons behind the murders and had a working title: *Beacon of Betrayal*.

35

November 5, 1952...Bonfire Night

Don't you Remember,
The Fifth of November,
'Twas Gunpowder Treason Day,
I let off my gun,
And made 'em all run.
And Stole all their Bonfire away.

Remember, remember, the fifth of November...

So went the popular little ditty from 1742.

Christopher Blaze had known where Gregory Montgomery was hiding out from the day he had returned from Serbia. They had spent many nights together after the evening performances ended and the curtain rung down. Certain things that Gregory said sent warning signals to his companion and he had fretted about it for days.

Gregory sat on the edge of his bed as Christopher ranted. The back of his head still throbbed with pain from being hit with the blunt end of a gun. He was actually even *more* upset about his severely bruised lip that would surely tarnish his good looks. As he had raced from Veronica's apartment a few days before, a garishly dressed woman with ruby red lips had approached him. He called her an extremely vulgar term, a slag, and was rewarded with a swift roundhouse punch to his face as she called him a wanker.

"Gregory," said Christopher Blaze as he paced nervously back and forth. "Listen, as you well know, we certainly don't see eye-to-eye on things political. I pay no attention to things like that anyway. Even with all the hubbub in the media about King George's death earlier this year, I was oblivious. I don't even know if Elizabeth has been crowned yet. Has she? Did I miss it?"

"You're an idiot, Christopher," blurted Gregory. "Frankly, you're as vacant and shallow as some of the roles you play. What's the point of this little lecture that's going nowhere?"

"Maybe I'm not as shallow as you think, dear boy. I've been picking up on certain tidbits of conversation here and there. I feel that you just might be involved in something nefarious. I don't know what, but I fear for your safety. Is someone after you for one reason or another?"

Silence from Gregory Montgomery. Just a cold stare.

"I mean it, Gregory. I just may notify the police I feel so fearful. I do so worry about you."

"That's *not* necessary, Christopher. You're letting your overly dramatic imagination run away with you. You're overacting, as you sometimes do. You worry needlessly. Shouldn't you be getting ready to head to the theater? It's matinee day today. Two performances and your mind will be cleared of all this nonsense. We'll talk about this later. Honestly, you're like a nervous old lady. There's nothing to worry about. Nothing. Run along, dear boy, run along."

Ten minutes later Christopher Blaze was on his way to the Drury Lane. Gregory picked up the telephone and dialed.

•

Devon listened as his caller tried foolishly to disguise his voice. Every time Devon started to speak further rambling cut him off. When there was finally a lull he said "But…"

But the call had ended.

He thought about the call for a brief moment and then picked up the phone once again and placed another call.

He glanced at his watch thirty minutes later and climbed his stairs carrying a cup of hot tea. Opening the door to his garden terrace he looked up at the clear blue sky. He walked over to a comfortable chair under one of the small trees he had growing up there. His neighbor was on his rooftop as well and they waved to each other.

Five minutes later Devon saw what he was waiting for. A lone pigeon glided overhead, circled and came to a stop, perching on top of his neighbor's aviary. The man approached the bird, gently stroking its head and back as he untied a small capsule from one of the bird's legs. Devon stood up, walking toward the short wall separating the two houses. Taking hold of the capsule, the man approached Devon, tossing the capsule to him as they got closer. Devon caught it one-handed, giving his friend a thumbs-up, and ran back downstairs.

As he sat next to his telephone, he unrolled the small typed note that had been inside the capsule and smiled as he read it.

This is to confirm your Intel. Affirmative.
Bonnymead Arms, cottage 7,
4901 Coltsfoot Circle, Ratfyn

Once again, he picked up the telephone and placed a call.

Devon Stone listened as the phone rang three times before being picked up on the other end.

"I just received a supposedly anonymous phone call a little over an hour ago. He was frantic and tried to disguise his voice. Certain speech patterns are…well, memorable, to say the least. I could tell right off that it was Christopher Blaze."

He listened as the voice at the other end spoke.

"Yes, yes. I know. That much we can assume by now," he said chuckling. "I'm sure their fans are oblivious. Anyway, he has very obviously misinterpreted things that Montgomery had been saying, and is of the belief that I am one of *them*. How he got my phone number is anybody's guess but who knows what kind of information the lot of them have on us. He told me where Gregory was staying. He thought that perhaps I could offer him some safe harbor, I suppose. What a fool. That information has just been verified. Amazing how quickly information can fly when you know just the right people. As luck would have it, my friend, Montgomery is staying at a small, out of the way guest lodge not too far from where you might be at the moment."

He listened again. Then he mentioned the name of the facility and the address.

"I figured you might like to be the one this time. Considering your personal involvement. Please, take care just in case this is a trap to lure one of us in. Happy hunting, and good luck."

•

Two hours after Christopher Blaze had left him Gregory heard a soft knocking on the door. Only two people knew where he was: Mildred Winsom and Christopher. He knew that it wouldn't be Mildred. He had called her as soon as Christopher left for the theater and sent her on a task. Christopher must have either forgotten something or had a change of heart about the whole situation. He glanced at his watch. He put down the damp cloth he had been using to dab his swollen lip. *That damn Blaze,* he thought, *should be at the theater by now!*

Without giving it a second thought he carelessly, foolishly, opened the door and was pushed back so abruptly that he fell backwards onto the floor, sending a shooting pain up his back. He let out a low yelp as he landed. His intruder immediately strode in, slamming the door behind him, and sat squarely on his chest, pinning him down while he forced a soaked cloth over the actor's face. He struggled as the pungent aroma worked its way into his brain and a sweet taste leaked between his lips. He tried to hold his breath but couldn't. Beginning to see strange, bright spiraling colors and hearing weird sounds, he weakened. It takes five minutes, at least, to render someone unconscious with chloroform.

•

When Gregory Montgomery regained consciousness, he couldn't move his arms or legs. For that matter, he could barely move at all. He looked around, discovering that he was sitting in a large wooden wheelbarrow, arms and legs trussed. He felt that there must be some sort of large floppy hat on his head. He knew that he was outdoors, in some dark out-of-the-way place, but he heard the happy shouting of crowds, somewhere way off in the distance, enjoying various bonfires. Fireworks were exploding as well. Then he noticed that he was surrounded in the wheelbarrow by straw. Lots of it. It was also tucked into his shirt and into his pants, which were unbuckled at the waist.

"Well, you have awakened, I see," said a soft voice from behind him.

It made him jump. As much as he could, considering the bounds. A shadowy figure walked around in front of him and bent down to face him. Because of the darkness, he still couldn't tell who it was.

"Good evening, Gregory," said Clovis James. "It's time for your final performance. Sure to be a roaring success. I may be forced to give you a rave review, how about that?"

"I don't understand. What's going on here? Are you insane?" asked the now trembling actor.

"Not insane, you miserable murderous bastard, just vengeful. I'm still in mourning for my sweet, loving Aunt Min."

Decades earlier, Clovis James had been the nephew who couldn't pronounce her first name, dubbing her forever afterwards: Min. Aunt Min to him. Little Min to all of her friends.

Gregory Montgomery was about to die and he knew it.

36

Billy and Peyton were suddenly acting like teenagers again, playing with firecrackers and enjoying the hijinks of countless dozens of other people up and down the streets around the building where Veronica's flat was located. It was still early in the evening and Veronica wouldn't be back from the theater for hours yet. They nonchalantly walked around the neighborhood, with nary a thought about any potential danger they might be in. Stopping to watch as one wheelbarrow after another was set ablaze with an effigy of Guy Fawkes within. They laughed right along with the little kids who lit the Flying Imps and sent them spinning off in any which direction, ducking and running when the exploding projectiles came straight at them. Roman candles were being sent aloft along the street, momentarily lighting the surroundings. Every few moments they would stop as Billy lit another firecracker and threw it into the air. A memory suddenly came flooding back and he laughed.

"Hey, Peyton, remember that Cabbage Night back in Dover when we were, what, maybe twelve?"

"Nope, we were thirteen. The first year that we could go out and do stupid stuff. And I know exactly where you're going with this."

"Yeah, right. What was her name? Marion something," asked Billy.

"Oh, I'll *never* forget," Peyton smirked, shaking his head. "Marion Fusinato. First girl in our class to grow tits. And whose brilliant idea was it to moon her through those big sliding glass doors on her back porch?"

"Well, I was *sure* that it was *her* sitting in that big chair near the windows. Anyway, it was *your* ugly hairy ass up against that window that caused the scream."

"Hey, hey, hey, I had a cute hairy ass. Still do for that matter," laughed Peyton, shaking his backside playfully toward Billy.

"Yeah, well, buddy, I'll just have to take your word for that. Once her mother let out that screech we bolted like hell, didn't we?"

"*You*, maybe. It ain't so easy trying to run like the wind and pull your pants up at the same damn time! I still go out of my way to avoid driving past her place. I nearly peed myself when her big old father came out of the house chasing us."

They nearly collapsed with laughter and Billy handed over some more fireworks for Peyton to ignite. Peyton lit one and threw it into the air. As it exploded he wondered what ever happened to Marion Fusinato? For the briefest of moments they had forgotten that possibly someone was still chasing them. With deadly intents.

The air was filled with smoke from the fires, the noise from hundreds of firecrackers going off all around them, shrieks of laughter from kids of all ages, as the two long-time friends meandered back to Veronica's flat with fond memories in their heads. It seemed such a long time ago.

37

As much as he struggled, there was no way that Gregory could get free. When he tried to call out for help, an old dirty rag had been stuffed into his mouth, which was then tied securely around his head by a rough, scratchy cord. He could smell the burning wood from the distant fires as the smoke drifted in his direction. He could hear the joyful shouts and laughter. He could hear firecrackers and fireworks exploding nearby. Then, all of a sudden, he began to pick up another, familiar aroma. An aroma that made him panicky. His eyes widened in absolute fear. Actually it was more in terror. The new aroma was that of petrol. Diesel fuel. Clovis James started pouring the liquid from a large can around the base, then into the wheelbarrow and down the front of Gregory's shirt as he twisted and twisted in fright, his eyes about to pop out of his head.

Gregory tried to rock the wheelbarrow back and forth, hoping to tip it over. He realized, of course, that any attempts to escape were futile.

Clovis struck a small wooden match and held the tiny flame aloft.

Then he blew it out, throwing it to the ground.

He watched the expression on Gregory's face, now contorted in abject horror, as difficult to hear squeals of anguish tried to come from Gregory's mouth. Clovis struck another match and started to walk toward the wheelbarrow. He blew *that* one out.

"I'm not a torturer, Gregory," said James, shaking his head. "No, I won't make you suffer. Too much. And look, I'm even giving you a standing ovation after all these years."

Gregory Montgomery could feel his heart racing faster and faster. He could feel the scream in his throat that couldn't come out of his gagged mouth. He could feel something hard that was roughly pressed to his chest. The barrel of a pistol. And then Gregory Montgomery could no longer feel anything once his sternum shattered and a bullet pierced his heart.

Clovis James struck another match. He did not blow it out.

And then there was one.

It would be years, if ever, before the charred remains of Gregory Montgomery, famous stage actor, Nazi sympathizer, brutal assassin, might be found buried deeply beneath a large, old, abandoned tomato garden, behind the cottage once belonging to a well admired, much read, revenge-seeking theater critic in the quaint village of Amesbury, the "Home of Stonehenge".

38

Mildred Winsom didn't get nervous very often. But she was *very* nervous at the moment. She was expecting to hear back from both Gregory and Edna about their successes in the ridding of one more of their opposing assassins and that nosey Veronica Barron. There would surely be celebrations amongst her associates in the killing of Devon Stone. The world would mourn the death of a much-loved author, and the theater world would be minus one more talent but they'd both be soon forgotten. And then her little band could continue to track down the remaining witches unencumbered.

True, she had been upset, initially, when Edna had told her that she was going to do the deed with Stone. Mildred had hoped that she would be the one to sever his handsome head from his body. But time was wasting and Stone was getting far too close to achieving *his* goals.

She was hesitant about calling Edna Vanderhoff at home, not wanting to talk to her inspector husband, but it was midday and he should be off doing whatever he did. She dialed Edna's number and waited as the phone rang six times. She was about to hang up when a man's voice answered. She quickly pressed the plunger with a finger ending the call.

Although she and Gregory Montgomery had been staying in separate rooms in the same ratty guesthouse, she had recently moved on to another such place a few miles away. She sat mulling over the situation for a few minutes. Realizing that it may be foolhardy, she gathered her coat and pocketbook, got into her car and drove to the place where she and Gregory had last stayed.

●

"He's *gone*, missy," said the woman at the front desk of Gregory's hideout when Mildred had very rudely asked of his whereabouts.

"What do you mean by that?" asked an agitated Mildred Winsom.

"Do I need to spell it out for ya?" responded the now cranky frizzy-haired old woman behind the desk as she stubbed out her cigarette and peered at Mildred over the top of her glasses. "All I know is that he's gone. Haven't seen him nor heard him, although I thought I heard a bit of a ruckus a couple hours ago and I went out to check on it. Left his room in a shambles," the woman continued, putting the book down that she had been reading. "His door was standing wide open, the place was a mess, but looks like his clothes are still there. There was a big stain of some kind on the rug, too. Smelled like piss, if you ask me. I hope the bloke hasn't skipped out because he still owes me for the week. I closed his door again and came back here."

"That makes no sense," Mildred said.

"What doesn't?" asked the woman. "Me telling you or him skipping out?"

The dark, dank, dingy little room where they were talking reeked of cigarette smoke and a cat's litter box that obviously had not been cleaned out in several days.

Without saying a further word, Mildred turned on her heals, left the woman and went back outside. It was still early, not yet dark. People had already started shooting off firecrackers and fireworks not too far away. The noise irritated her even more than she was already. She had been extremely concerned when she had knocked repeatedly on Gregory's door with no response from within. Because his car was still parked where she had last seen it.

Now Mildred Winsom was even *more* nervous. And, worse, she was furious. And desperate. She got back into her car and drove straight back into London. If she had to wait all night, she was going to kill *someone*. Maybe a few someones. And she knew their location.

•

Billy and Peyton were within a few paces of Veronica's building when it happened. The popping of firecrackers and shouts of laughter concealed the gunshot. Peyton dropped to the ground, clutching his left shoulder. Billy thought that his friend was playing around, trying to be funny. He changed his mind as soon as he saw the blood oozing from between his friend's fingers.

They were both wearing bomber jackets. They had been walking away from her. Mildred Winsom couldn't tell which one she had hit; she only knew that one of them dropped to the ground. Was it the smoker or his friend? She had tried aiming at the person's head but it was too dark. She couldn't tell where, exactly, the man had been struck. The one not hit stooped down anxiously to look at his friend and then made a mad dash into the building. There were people further away, out and about in the street, but she thought no one else had seen the man drop. Would she have enough time to finish off the fallen man, if he wasn't already dead? Looking around to make sure she was unseen, she stepped from behind the tree...her hiding place...and slowly, cautiously walked toward the fallen man.

39

Despite the confusion and noises of the festive evening, and despite what Mildred had first thought, others near the scene *had* watched the man fall to the ground. A few concerned revelers began to run forward as Mildred Winsom quickly stepped backward. Back into the shadows. The piercing sound of an ambulance siren drew closer. Billy had rushed back outside to kneel by his friend. He carefully removed Peyton's bomber jacket and his shirt, now oozing with blood.

"Hang in there, buddy," Billy whispered. "Please hang in there."

Mildred Winsom gritted her teeth and slinked further back into the trees, further into the shadows. *If it hadn't been so dark. If she had had a better line of vision. If she had been swift enough. If she hadn't been so careless.* If. If. If. Too many ifs.

Mildred knew that she had, indeed, gotten careless and sloppy. Her vengeful anger and bloodlust had taken over and clouded her every move.

But at least *one* of them was down. And he wasn't moving.

•

A Bobby had been close to the scene, rushing up as soon as the ambulance arrived. He started asking a lot of questions. Billy had no

179

answers. At least not any answers appropriate enough to give to the police at this time. More police cars began to arrive.

By the time the ambulance had arrived, Peyton was sitting up, his bomber jacket, shirt, and T-shirt removed, with Billy applying pressure to assuage the bleeding as much as he could. He had pressed Peyton's T-shirt into the wound, which had helped to some degree.

The first responders made a rapid assessment, determining the next course of action. Aside from speeding him to the hospital. The bullet had torn through Peyton's very muscular left shoulder, apparently not hitting any bones and then made a clean but bloody exit wound. They dressed the wounds, front and back, and hastened him onto a stretcher and into the ambulance. Before Billy could say anything, the ambulance sped away, the slowly diminishing sound of the siren announcing its departure. Billy watched in helpless anguish as it disappeared down the street.

"So," a police officer started questioning Billy, "you have no idea who may have shot your friend?"

"No, sir, none whatsoever," answered Billy. "My friend and I are here in London visiting with my girlfriend who happens to live in this building. We were just out enjoying all the excitement of the holiday and headed back in for the night."

"I guess your friend was sort of lucky that he was wearing that heavy leather jacket," said the officer. "May have lessened the severity."

"Please," said Billy plaintively, "is there any way I can get to the hospital with my friend? I have no idea where they're taking him."

A small group of concerned revelers had formed by this time.

"I think I saw her," called out a teenager amongst the gathered crowd. He pointed to a stand of trees between the building and the street. "I was sure I saw someone fire a gun from behind that one over there."

"Are you sure, lad?" asked the first Bobby who had arrived at the scene following the shooting. "It's awfully dark around here."

"Yes, sir, I swear," answered the young man. "I sneaked into the trees to take a piss and that's when I heard the gunshot. Scared me and I jumped, wetting my trousers a little, I did. She didn't see me, though. I hope."

The Bobby smiled at that.

"I think she also had a knife, but I really couldn't swear to that," continued the teenager, now showing a bit of nervousness. "She was skinny and dressed all in black. I thought she was dressed up like a witch or something, y'know? Bloody hell, she looked bitchy mean."

"Now, now, watch your language son," admonished the Bobby. "There are ladies around here."

"Yes, sir. I'm sorry," answered the embarrassed young man.

The Bobby continued with the questioning but nothing further could be gained from the few remaining stragglers. The night began to seem quiet. No more firecrackers were being lit. No more fireworks exploding overhead.

At the first sound of the approaching ambulance, Mildred Winsom had cautiously, quietly fled the scene. Something had inadvertently slipped, unseen by her, from her handbag as she had first withdrawn her pistol. On the ground, beneath the tree, lay a small black and white Polaroid photograph of three young people exiting a theater. She had hoped to put a big red X-mark across all of their faces before the night ended. She was getting tired from all the running around but she suddenly remembered that she had told Gregory Montgomery that she would get to the Drury Lane Theater before Christopher Blaze left. It was getting late, but this might be a successful, deadly night after all.

The Bobby was very sympathetic, especially hearing that Billy and Peyton were life-long friends and had fought in the war together.

"I'll make sure you get to see your friend in hospital," said the friendly Bobby. "I hope he survives. I'll take you there myself."

40

The curtain had long since come down, the theater emptied, and most of the people behind the scenes had departed for the night. Christopher sat alone and still disconsolate in his dressing room. He sighed, got up, put on his coat, and gathered his hat and gloves. Turning out the light in his room and closing the door, he walked down the long dark hallway on the way out. He could see the glow from the ghost light burning center stage. The light that in theater legend keeps the evil spirits away or dancing, depending upon who tells the tale. Ironically, even though ghost lights are placed every evening in every theater around the globe, the Drury Lane Theater is famously known as the most haunted theater in the world. And the most famous ghost who walks these halls is the "Man in Grey", a knife-stabbed man whose skeletal remains were found within a walled-up passage in 1848.

Christopher exited through the stage door. He was surprised to see a lone fan waiting there.

"Ah, ha, there you are, at last, Mr. Blaze!" squealed the slender, dark-haired woman, with a bit of a Cockney accent. "I just *loved* the show and you were simply marvelous. Simply marvelous. Never laughed so much in me life! I had to wait, no matter how long, to get your autograph," she said as she handed him her playbill. "Would you mind?"

"My dear, dear woman, how wonderfully flattering," said the now ego-inflated actor. "I'm sorry I took my time coming out of the theater. To think that you waited so long for me, Miss...?"

"Oh, you can just call me Millie," the woman said as she reached into her over-sized pocketbook.

41

November 6, 1952

It was apparent that the body was quite dead, not merely because of the listless manner in which it was sprawled across the ground, arms and legs akimbo, but by the fact that it was also headless.

A thick fog, for which this city is famous, swirled around the buildings adding to the chill of the scene. A "pea-souper", as the Londoners say. The young police Inspector approached the gruesome sight very cautiously, not fearing the thing suddenly springing to life, but not wanting to disturb any potential, crucial evidence surrounding it. The back alley to the Drury Lane Theater had already been cordoned off with barricades. A dustman, come to dump the theater's trash bins, had been the first to spot the body. Thinking that it might be a dummy prop for a show or a leftover effigy of Guy Fawkes, he nonchalantly approached it, heading for the bins beyond it. When he stepped into a puddle of blood and saw the severed head, he realized the error in his first assessment and promptly fainted, hitting his head on the cobblestone pavement. Upon recovering, he ran to the red telephone booth at the entry to the alley to notify the police. Within minutes, the sirens were heard and several men in uniform soon joined him in the alley.

"Oh, dear, dear, dear," said the visibly shaken Inspector as he leaned over the dismembered corpse once again. "Pity. Poor man. Poor man."

He strolled several feet away where the severed head rested on its side, empty eyes looking skyward. A blood-splattered playbill lay beneath the head. The Inspector cocked his own head and could make out, through the mess, the autograph: *Dearest Millie, your kind words have given me a swollen head. Warmest regards, Christopher Blaze.*

Due to the troublesome situation outside the theater and the loss now of not one but two of their leading men...one to a heinous murder, and one completely vanishing without a trace...the producers of *Private Lives* elected to suspend performances until further notice.

42

By midmorning a brisk breeze cleared away the fog and picked up a small black and white photograph from under a stand of large, old trees blowing it out to the middle of the sidewalk. A very tired, garishly dressed red-haired woman of indeterminate age with smeared red lipstick saw whatever it was being blown and bent down to pick it up. Delores, ne Agnes, looked at it, brushing off the few little pieces of dirt clinging to it. She recognized the woman in the photo, an actress, and was intrigued by those two handsome men. She was sure she had seen one of them around this area before. She did *not* notice the blood stains on the sidewalk leading up to the building in front of which she was now standing. She was about to throw the photograph back down onto the ground when a taxicab pulled up to the curb.

A very tired-looking and distraught Veronica and Billy stepped out onto the sidewalk. They had just left the hospital and their friend Peyton. Their nerves were frazzled. Billy paid the cabbie and sent him on his way. Then they saw Delores standing there, staring at them.

"Good morning, ducky," Delores said to Billy, giving him a huge smile and a wink. "Night out on the town, eh? Bet it was a noisy one, eh?" And she laughed a wheezy smokers kind of laugh.

"Hello, Delores," Veronica said coolly. "Not exactly what you might be thinking."

Veronica and Billy turned to go into the building when Delores called out to them.

"Wait, I found something just now. Is this yours?" she asked as she handed the photograph to them.

They scrutinized the photo and each one had a puzzled look on their faces.

"Where did you get this, Delores?" asked Veronica. "Did you take this picture?"

"Oh, no, missy. 'T'wasn't me. I ain't got a camera. It was on the ground. Musta been over there," she said, pointing to the trees. "The wind picked it up and blew it at me feet not five minutes ago."

A chill ran up Billy's back. Those were the trees that the teenager had said the shooter was hiding behind last night.

•

It took several attempts to reach him, but when Devon Stone finally answered his telephone Billy Bennett tried to control his anger.

"Good afternoon, Devon," Billy said while clenching and unclenching a fist. "This is Billy, by the way. I want to say this as calmly as I can but it won't be easy."

"All right, Billy," answered Devon with a furrowed brow and concern in his voice. "Has something happened to either you or Veronica?"

"No. Not exactly. But it could have. It could have been very bad. My friend Peyton was shot last night out in front of Veronica's building. It turned out to be non-life threatening, and he's still in the hospital for a day or so, but..."

"My God, man, that's horrendous!" exclaimed Devon. "Could it have been accidental? You know, because of all the nonsense going on with Bonfire Night?"

"I seriously doubt it, Devon. I really *seriously* doubt it," answered Billy.

Billy explained about the teenager's story about witnessing a female shooter and then about the photograph that was found near the scene.

"I know now, Devon, that the three of us seemingly innocent bystanders in your cause are in the crosshairs of one of those assassins you're seeking.

Peyton and I have certainly been targets before, obviously, during the war. But this is a new, extremely frightening experience for poor Ronnie."

"Ronnie?" asked Devon.

"Sorry. That's Veronica," answered Billy.

"Just to let you know, Billy," Devon continued, still shaken from the news, "I believe there is only one remaining name to be crossed off our list. That name is Mildred Winsom's so that witness may have been absolutely correct."

Billy was silent for a moment.

"Peyton brought an entire arsenal with him when he first came from home. I'd be more than willing to riddle her with all the bullets possible," Billy said through gritted teeth.

"Careful there, my friend," Devon said, shaking his head. "No, you must not...*can* not be involved in her killing. The three of you must be completely removed from anything that could end in your incarceration. No, it must be either myself, Anoushka or Clovis. You must remain totally innocent...although, unfortunately, you *are* complicit."

"But..." stammered Billy.

"No buts about it, Billy. There cannot be any blood on your hands. Well, okay, so we all realize that you've lied to the police a few times recently. You've witnessed a murder and you may very well witness another. But what the authorities *don't* know can't hurt you, right?"

Billy sighed in acquiescence.

"So, leave Peyton's arsenal safe and sound at Veronica's place. Get it back to the States unused," Devon said, trying to calm his friend. "Mildred is cunning, to be sure. But she's getting sloppy. She must be getting desperate. She will start to do very stupid things. I've written about such behavior in several of my novels."

Billy had to chuckle at that comment. *This is not made up fiction*, he thought, *this is real life...and death.*

"I'll see what I can come up with as soon as I can, Billy. I assure you that Mildred's days are numbered. Please, *please* give my warmest regards to Veronica…may I call her Ronnie? And to Peyton, with hope for a hasty, healthy recovery. You two are very brave men and I've grown very fond of you. All three of you, actually."

And Devon Stone ended the call abruptly.

43

"I have a plan," announced Devon Stone when Veronica answered her telephone. "Please listen very carefully. Very. Carefully."

And she did.

44

Mildred Winsom was hoping that she would be able to get at Devon Stone on the street where he lived. He hadn't left his house in days. She couldn't just go up to his door and knock. He now knew what she looked like. But if he would just come out of his house as she drove by, one gunshot would do it. Every day she slowly drove past his house shortly after the evening papers were delivered. Surely he'd step out to get it. She drove past the house, then around the long block. She did this three times in a row. It took seven minutes between each pass. She would then drive off to wherever her hiding place might be and try again the next day. She didn't really want to risk doing anything carelessly foolish causing failure but she was getting more frustrated as the days went by. Maybe she'd have to change to something more drastic. But for now, she continued her daily drives.

This had not gone unnoticed. And monitored.

As she was slowly driving toward his house for the third time, his front door suddenly opened. She saw that there was a vacant parking space directly behind a shiny hunter-green car. She pulled into it and waited. But it wasn't Devon Stone who emerged. It was the woman who Mildred, weeks ago, had thought was the Night Witch. She was the one who had murdered her lover, Jacob Everett. Close behind her was Veronica Barron. *What luck*, she thought. *I can shoot them both and Devon, too, when he comes running out to help.*

They actually looked frightened for some reason as they rushed down the front steps. It was a miserable drizzly afternoon and the two women put up a large umbrella and walked hurriedly, arm in arm, up the sidewalk, away from her car. She was just about to step out of her car when Devon immediately appeared at his front door. Mildred's jaw dropped. She was incredulous. He raised his arm, pointing a pistol at the two women. He fired a shot and the Russian woman fell to the ground. Veronica, with fear in her eyes, turned to see her fallen companion and Devon fired again. Veronica arched her back, clutched her chest and crumpled to the ground.

What the hell did I just witness? Mildred's mind was frazzled as she slowly stepped from her car. She started walking toward them. But something was off. Something was not quite right. She pulled her own pistol from her handbag and slowly raised it. No movement but there was no blood. Neither woman appeared to be bleeding anywhere. She lowered her pistol and stared in confusion.

Billy, who had run out of the house and had been hiding in Devon Stone's beautiful car since Mildred's first pass around the block, slowly rolled down a window. Lighting one of his remaining firecrackers, the loud Jumping Cracker, he tossed it at Mildred's feet. It exploded, causing her to scream and drop her gun. Anoushka and Veronica immediately popped straight up, standing and staring Mildred right in the face.

"Surprise!" shouted Billy, right behind her.

"*Syurpriz!*" laughed Anoushka in Russian.

"Here's *another* surprise," shouted Veronica as she punched Mildred in the face, breaking the woman's nose.

But Mildred was vicious and desperate and certainly *not* ready to bring the situation to an unsatisfactory end just yet. She kicked out at Anoushka, roughly pushing her aside abruptly, and shoved Veronica back, making her trip over the dropped umbrella and fall. Veronica twisted her ankle in doing so and let out a little whimper of pain. Billy rushed to help her up as Mildred took off running. She didn't know where she would go but she just had to escape. And fast.

She ran up the street, heading toward Hampstead Heath. A place with thousands trees. At least a place to hide. Perhaps.

After a momentary hesitation, Anoushka started chasing after her. As soon as Billy got Veronica back up on her feet, assuring that nothing had been broken, he started following the two women up the hill toward wherever they might be running.

45

The earlier drizzle had now turned to a steady rain; and they kept running, kept chasing Mildred the murderer. The weather was keeping the Heath, normally filled with people on beautiful afternoons, almost empty and quiet. Mildred headed for an area that was more densely wooded, hoping to evade her pursuers. Anoushka had a small pistol with her but was hesitant to use it, fearing the gunshot would draw attention from anyone who might be out in the foul weather. She had seen a pedestrian walking his dog off in the distance but aside from him no one else seemed to be close by. The only weapon Billy had on him was that blasted knife that Peyton had brought in his arsenal. Why he had tucked it into his jacket pocket at the last minute before leaving the flat hours ago was a mystery to him, *but what the heck*, he had thought. He had proudly shown it to everyone at the house a couple hours ago as Devon carefully laid out the plans for the surprise awaiting Mildred.

Although he had used a suppressor when firing blanks at the two women, Billy was surprised that the noise from Devon's pistol, no matter how muffled, didn't draw neighbors out of their houses.

They ran through the park, darting between large stands of trees, and although she was fast, Billy and Anoushka seemed to be gaining on her. She was not that far ahead now. Billy lost his footing a couple times on the slick, wet terrain but Anoushka kept going like a gazelle.

Devon had sprinted from his house in hot pursuit of the trio but he knew, as spry as he was, his running was no match for the three younger people dashing up the street. He picked up Mildred's dropped gun, handing it to Veronica and hastily told her to get back into his house and wait for them all to return. Hoping, of course, that they would *all* return. Obviously Mildred appeared to be heading toward Hampstead Heath and perhaps the safety of hiding amongst the trees and bushes. *She must be desperate*, he thought. *She can run and maybe she can hide but for how long?*

As part of the plan to lure and capture Mildred, he had parked his car in a space directly in front of his house instead of putting it away in the gated parking area. He grabbed his keys, cranked the engine and shot out like a bullet toward the Heath. The plan wasn't turning out *exactly* as he had hoped, but he was sure that Mildred would soon be down, one way or another. Capturing her alive had been his original plan, but now he didn't care. As long as she was put out of commission permanently. He caught sight of the trio running as though pursued by a pride of lions down East Heath Road. Mildred veered off, racing into the park alongside Spaniards Road, followed closely by Anoushka and Billy. Devon turned the car onto Spaniards Road soon after. Still running as though she had the energy of an Olympian, Mildred crossed the road, dashing into a wooded area. Her fear of being caught and her adrenaline pushed her on, even though the muscles in her legs were on fire. She could taste the blood from her broken nose as it seeped into her mouth.

Devon then came to a fork in the road at that point. He stopped the car for a second, with the only sound being the rain hitting the rooftop and the swish-swish-swish of the windshield wipers. Should he continue on Spaniards Road or veer left onto North End Road? The Heath would be even less populated on that side of the park, even without the rain. On days with good weather, more activity would normally be at the opposite side. Mildred was probably aware of that fact and might use it to her advantage. He steered the car onto North End Road. He could see the trio running into and out of view as they raced through the shrubbery. Keeping his eye on the road and turning back and forth to the trio, *his* adrenaline was pulsing. All of a sudden he saw that they had entered a particularly dense part of the trees but had failed to emerge when the terrain opened up again. He stomped on the brakes and took the car out of gear.

Mildred had been wearing espadrilles and Billy and Anoushka came across a wet, muddy one as they ran. It was obvious to them that the woman had lost a shoe as she ran and must be slowing down as a result. They could see her just ahead, closer, but still running. They were so close they could hear her breathing, almost out of breath but still going.

"Your knife," Anoushka shouted to Billy as they ran. "Your knife. Do you still have it?"

Not slowing down, he pulled the knife from his pocket and withdrew it from its sheath. He held it out to her without slowing down for a second and she took hold of the blade. She held the blade by its end, stopped running for the briefest of seconds, pulled her arm back, and with the strongest of thrusts she could muster, she sent the knife spinning toward its intended target.

She had thrown a bit too high but gravity worked in their favor. No longer hearing footsteps running behind her, Mildred Winsom paused ever so slightly to turn to see where her followers were. It was the worst decision she had ever made in her life.

The spinning, speeding knife entered her right eye socket and the 9" blade penetrated straight into her brain. A look of shock and pain. She fell face first onto the muddy ground, pushing the blade even further into her skull.

Billy was stunned. He gazed at a satisfied-looking Anoushka, who now stood with her hands on her hips.
"*Yablochko!*" she shouted. "Bull's-eye!"
"Well, I'll be damned!" was all he could say.

And then there were none.

•

Fearing the worst, Devon pulled his car to the side of the road, grabbed the pistol that had been on the seat beside him, got out of the car and locked it. What with the noise of the rain and the windshield wipers, he hadn't heard any gunshots. If he had, though, who would be doing the shooting? He slowly started walking to the area in which he had last seen the pursuit. His eyes widened as he saw Anoushka leaning lazily against a tree. He quickened his pace. He didn't see Billy. Or Mildred Winsom.

As he got closer he could see Billy leaning down over something on the ground. Then Devon saw what that something was.

"Bloody hell," he exclaimed.

"Bloody hell is right," answered Billy, holding his knife. "I think my blade is bent!"

No further explanation required at that time, the trio lifted the deceased and walked, arms over shoulders, as a friendly foursome, toward Devon's car. No one was around on this rainy afternoon to notice that the feet of one of this odd group weren't even touching the ground, or that something very horrible had happened to her right eye and her nose was broken. Devon unlatched the boot of his car and they carefully laid the permanently silenced body inside. Devon winked at Anoushka as he quickly closed the boot.

"Your car is amazing, Devon," Billy exclaimed matter-of-factly along with a low whistle, as he stood back examining the car. "I've thought about it ever since that picnic by the cliffs. Can I drive it sometime?"

Devon Stone smiled but ignored the question as they all got into the car and drove slowly away.

Vera Lynn was singing on the car radio: *We'll meet again, don't know where, don't know when...*

And so, Mildred Winsom became just another name amongst the hundreds of other missing persons throughout England. But, at this point, there was no one left to care.

•

Devon Stone had realized that what he was going to be suggesting was very risky, to say the least. But, not unlike Mildred Winsom, he was getting frustrated that this situation was dragging on for too long without a viable conclusion. Death for one of them, his or Mildred's, was inevitable. But for which one? He had formulated his plan while thinking about the basic plot for his new book. Rejecting the idea at first, he mulled it over in his head before calling Veronica and Anoushka to see how they might feel about the ruse. The young Russian immediately thought the idea was a clever one and was ready to go. She, like her late, beloved sister, would be more than willing to climb out onto that wing to release the bombs, figuratively speaking. Veronica, on the other hand, had been hesitant. Billy wanted to be the one, instead of Veronica, to be part of the plot. Devon explained why that wouldn't be as effective, although the argument was fairly lame. The truth was, that it could go horribly wrong very quickly because of Mildred's unpredictability and violent temper.

The fact that a few years earlier, as an acting student, Veronica Barron had been taught how to fall realistically if her character had been shot played very nicely into Devon's plan. Although the others had been oblivious, Devon also had known that, prior to becoming a barmaid and a fellow-assassin, Anoushka Markarova had been an actress at the famed Moscow Pushkin Drama Theatre. That's how she had achieved an almost too-perfect British accent. She *also* knew how to fall realistically upon being shot. Her expert marksmanship she had learned on her own.

46

Two Nights Later

A cold, misty drizzle chilled the late evening air but Billy and Veronica paid no attention to the weather. They strolled, hand in hand, under a large umbrella. With her nights free, at least temporarily, they decided to play the tourist again, albeit cautiously. Devon had assured them that all the dangers seemed to be behind them, yet they were still apprehensive. She had promised to do something with him since his first night's arrival. Certain unforeseen circumstances had intervened but now the time was right.

They slowly ambled up Whitehall, with Veronica pointing out Westminster Abbey.

"That's where Elizabeth will become Queen Elizabeth next year. Actually, Elizabeth became queen as soon as her father passed away, but her *official* coronation won't take place until next June. I have no doubt the celebrations will go on for days. The Brits love their royalty."

"Why wait so long for the coronation?" asked Billy.

"Out of respect for the death of her father. A proper mourning period for one thing, and it takes a long time to prepare for all the pomp and circumstance of a coronation for another thing."

Billy leaned into her and kissed her on the cheek.

"You're *my* princess, Ronnie. You're *my* royalty," he whispered.

"Oh, stop," laughed Veronica, "That's infantile and *way* too mushy.

You sound like a lovesick teenager. Not up to your standard. I think I told you this once before. You need a better scriptwriter."

And she pushed him, almost making him fall into the gutter.

Their destination was on Bridge Street. A bell tower with the most famous bell in the world: Big Ben. When it was completed in 1859 it was the largest and most accurate four-faced chiming clock in the world. Veronica pointed out that fact and that all four nations of the United Kingdom were represented on the tower: a rose for England, a thistle for Scotland, a shamrock for Ireland, and a leek for Wales. Billy was impressed by Veronica's knowledge.

"See, I'm not just an addle-brained actress," she said, sticking out her tongue playfully.

"Could have fooled *me*," he teased.

This time she pushed him hard enough that he *did* fall into the gutter.

Somewhere nearby a car backfired. Veronica screamed and Billy ducked. They looked at each and laughed until they were crying. They shared a large Cadbury chocolate bar as they continued their stroll and waited for Big Ben to strike midnight.

47

The Next Day: Time For Goodbyes

Peyton and Anoushka were lying side by side in what was, up until recently, her bedroom in Veronica's flat. He was on his back; she lay on her stomach, propped up on one of her elbows. She was playfully, lazily drawing figure eights through his chest hair, encircling his rigid nipples with her fingertips. Avoiding the bandage covering his recent shoulder wound, she gently caressed a wartime scar a bit lower on his abdomen, slightly below his navel. The recent dramatic and deadly situation seems not to have left any permanent *emotional* scars, evidently.

"Careful where you're going there, kiddo," he whispered, looking down toward her hand. "You could get yourself into trouble if you don't watch out."

She giggled, nibbled him on an earlobe and let her hand slip a bit lower. And then a bit lower.

She got herself into trouble. Twice.

•

Two hours later, a soft tapping on the bedroom door awakened Peyton.

"Hate to disturb you, buddy, but Devon wants us to swing by his place before we head to the airport. Veronica will meet us there. She's rehearsing

her show now with the replacement for those two other guys. Hustle! Pack
your gear and bring it with us. We'll go right to the airport from there."

Peyton slowly rolled over and caressed Anoushka on her back.
"Hey, gorgeous, we have…"
"Yes, I heard him," cooed the young assassin, with a broad smile as
she, too, rolled over.
"Promise you'll come to the States as soon as you can? I think we might
have something going here, don't you?"
"We *do*, oh yes, I agree," she shrugged her shoulders. "I would love to
see much more of you," and she giggled girlishly after that remark. "You
know what I mean. It didn't come out right. A major problem exists at
the moment, though. You keep forgetting that I am a Soviet citizen. With
the Cold War going on and my country siding with the North Koreans
at this point, I wouldn't actually be greeted with open arms. Unless I can
somehow get a fake passport, I am essentially barred from entering your
country. I had to get special permission to come here to England. It wasn't
easy."

Peyton scrunched up his face and thought about it for a second or two.
"Come on, let's go. We'll see about that. After all, don't we have friends
in high places?"

•

Veronica arrived at Devon Stone's residence at the precise moment he
was popping the cork on the second bottle of Dom Perignon Oenotheque
Brut Millesime.
Billy held up the first, empty bottle and studied the label.
"I sure as hell can't pronounce it, but this stuff sure goes down easy!"
"Ahh, and there's the queen of the London stage at the moment.
Welcome, my dear, come join the party," Devon said as he greeted Veronica.
"How did your rehearsal go? Is that replacement any good?"

Clovis James almost choked on his champagne when he heard that.
After winning the Tony Award in New York earlier in the year, José Ferrer

had been signed to complete the run of *Private Lives*. Once a Limited Engagement, it was now extended indefinitely.

"Oh, he'll do, I suppose," Veronica teased, winking at Clovis.

"Well, cheers to everyone," said Devon, raising his freshly filled glass and presenting one to Veronica. "Personally, I'm sad to see you two boys head for home. I know this hasn't been the most pleasant of...well... adventures, now, has it?"

"Let's just say that the thrill was a bit different than the ones we experienced in and over Germany a few years back," answered Billy. "My buddy, here, and I *do* have a business to run back home. If his dad and cousin haven't already burned the place down in our absence, or killed each other. For me, Mr. Stone, I've grown quite fond of you. I may have to start reading your books now."

Devon smiled.

"I hope so, young man. I sincerely hope so. Don't be surprised if you happen to recognize some familiar traits and personalities in a character or two in my next thriller," he said winking broadly. "How about you, Peyton, have you read any of my books yet?"

"Are you kidding?" interjected Billy. "His favorite reading material consists of thin flimsy things with colorful drawings of Flash Gordon or Superman."

"Hey," said Peyton, hands on hips with a defiant look, "don't forget Archie and Jughead!"

Devon laughed, shaking his head, and offered them a tray of hors d'oeuvres, which contained slices of various cheeses and cold meats. And, similar to that picnic luncheon they had all enjoyed along the White Cliffs, there were slices of that bread with the crisp, crunchy golden crust. Billy looked at the tray and backed away from the cheese that reminded him of horse poop.

The conversation drifted from the casual pleasantries to the unpleasant situation that the three Americans had been brought into almost by accident and definitely *not* by plan. Apologies came from not only Devon, but from Anoushka and Clovis as well.

"Okay, so we know from what you've just told us," Peyton began, "that you were able to formulate your…hmmm…hit list, as it were, from your sources at MI6. But how were those other guys able to get their *own* hit list and start killing off *your* team?"

"Logical question, young man," answered Devon. "We finally determined, later in the game, that there was actually a mole amongst us. Suspicions were aroused when one person in particular was eliminated. Our planning had been too precise in one situation and the death of an ally took us by surprise. Again, MI6 came through and we, in turn, eliminated that turncoat. And, as it turned out, it was sheer happenstance that Winsom and I, captains of our teams as it were, lived two doors apart. I don't know if that worked in anyone's favor or not. We can't ask Mildred's opinion of that now, can we?"

"This is all too much for my mind to handle," said Veronica shaking her head. "I had assumed that the war was over and far behind us. That shows how terribly naïve I am."

"Sadly," said Devon, "the war is never over. No matter what year, no matter which war. True, the murders of the Night Witches have ceased. But, who knows? There are still those who harbor hatred. And will do so until their dying days. They might not fly Nazi flags from their rooftops, but they still conceal their political beliefs. It will resurface again sometime in the future, I have no doubt."

He paused and *almost* considered refraining from saying anything further, but then continued.

"Look at your *own* country, the three of you," he said nodding to the American trio. "I've traveled all over the United States, as a tourist and as a writer doing research for my books. Is the Civil War really and truly over? Traveling through your deep south I've seen the Confederate flag waving proudly. I've heard old folks speaking of the war of northern aggression.

I've seen the 'Whites Only' and 'Colored Only' signs everywhere. Change *will* come. Eventually. I hope. Alas, no country is immune to prejudice. *There is no education like adversity*."

"Is that another Churchill quote or from one of your books?" asked Peyton.

"No, actually it was in a fortune cookie from my Chinese takeout last week," laughed Devon. "I was gobsmacked when I read it and found that very intriguing, because that quote is from Benjamin Disraeli. They're hiring a better quality of fortune cookie writers these days, to be sure!"

"Well, enough is enough, Stone," said Clovis James, shaking his head and bringing his hands together in one loud clap. "I was hoping for some *lighter* conversation at this point. This should be a celebration today, not a dirge."

"Of course, my friend. The lovable critic here is absolutely correct. Please forgive my lecture on humanity. We should, indeed, be rejoicing that this mystery has been resolved."

"Now that you mention that word 'mystery'," Billy said, "We have a slight confession that will lead to a mystery that has perplexed Veronica and me for weeks."

"And that would be...?" Devon asked as he glanced back and forth between the two.

Veronica cleared her throat and proceeded to tell Devon the entire story about their encroachment into Mildred Winsom's house, their narrow rooftop escape, and their viewing of an unfriendly neighbor coming from the basement door a mere few feet from where they had been hiding and where they were all standing at the present time.

"And," she continued, almost breathless at this moment, "we saw a strange glowing light coming up from the basement. What's going on down there?"

Billy, Veronica, and Peyton stood staring at Devon Stone as he rocked back in uncontrollable laughter, tears flowing down his cheeks.

"That is way too funny. It seems as though *you* two have just solved a mystery that has been puzzling that neighbor for weeks on end. He was clearly convinced that he had heard running footsteps coming from above while he was in the basement. But when he came up, nobody was around. Regarding that glow?"

He cleared his throat and paused, perhaps for dramatic effect.

"Well, London weather is not conducive to growing some particular plants outdoors. Certain plants require a specific amount of light to produce what is expected of them. A grow light, for example, is needed in place of sunlight. By any chance, are you at all familiar with Cannabis?"

"You mean Mary Jane?…Weed?…Whacky tabacky?" asked Peyton, wide-eyed.

"I figured *you*, of all people, would certainly know about it," chuckled Devon. "But, please. Don't call the authorities just yet, however. I'm not a dealer. I grow it strictly for personal…ummm…*medicinal* purposes only. You'd be amazed at how my senses are heightened when I'm smoking and writing. Why, the words just *flow* like a river at times! It's quite relaxing, as well. I may offer you some to quell your jittery nerves, if you'd like. Oh, and it is simply *wonderful* cooked in certain dishes if prepared properly. Yes, my good neighbor was watering them and tending to them when you were playing 'hide and seek' or 'catch me if you can' with the dearly departed Mildred."

Devon turned as he heard someone approaching from behind him, coming from the kitchen. The man was carrying a serving platter covered with a small silver dome.

Billy and Veronica froze.

"Peyton, Billy, and Veronica…and *especially* Billy and Veronica… I'd like you to meet my good friend and next door neighbor."
It was that cantankerous elderly man with the rumpled grey hair.
"I am honored to introduce you to Chester Davenport."

"Oh, it's *you* two again, is it?" Said the man, this time with a huge smile and a lecherous wink at Veronica.

"Chester Davenport? *The* Chester Davenport?" Peyton asked in astonishment. "The retired director of MI6?"

"At your service, sir," said Davenport with a slight bow.

He held out the serving platter, slowly lifting the dome.

"Care to try one of my very *special* brownies?" he asked with a twinkle in his eye. "Freshly baked this morning. I'm sure you'll find them quite… umm, refreshing."

Epilogue

A little more than three weeks after Billy and Peyton had returned home to New Jersey, another disaster hit London. It lasted for five days. Because of a combination of a period of unusually cold weather causing Londoners to burn more coal to heat their homes, and stagnant, windless air not moving at all over the city, a thick layer of choking, deadly smog settled over the area. It reduced visibility far worse than any "normal" London fog and even penetrated into indoor areas. Public transport ceased because of the poor visibility, which meant that there was no air movement caused by traffic. Reports estimated that upwards of four thousand people had died as a direct result and over one hundred thousand more were made severely ill. Those affected the worst were the elderly and the very young, and those with pre-existing respiratory conditions. When the weather suddenly changed, the deadly smog dispersed quickly. But the effects lingered. Among the deceased was Police Inspector Howard Vanderhoff, who had still held out hope that his missing wife, Edna, would soon return home.

Devon Stone worked this killer fog into the book he had just begun writing, creating a more sinister, disturbing setting for a couple of his murders.

Eight months later, the book *Beacon of Betrayal* now published, became

Devon's most successful, fastest selling thriller to date. He sent a signed copy to Billy Bennett with a personal inscription.

Billy Bennett was delighted to receive the book and was proud to see that it had been dedicated to three brave Americans (anonymous, for obvious reasons). Upon reading it, he couldn't stop laughing when a character he recognized as having *very* familiar, personal traits had turned from being quite likable at the beginning of the book to actually being revealed as the murderer in the shocking, surprise twist of an ending.

Veronica Barron graciously turned down the role in a new musical written especially for her by Noel Coward. She simply did not like the script and found the music bland and not up to his usual standards, although she declined to tell that to the famous author. When the show finally *did* open in the West End, the critics roundly trounced it, with a particularly withering review from Clovis James.

Noel Coward wrote a blistering letter to the critic, verbally accusing him of, among other things, being a hateful hack writer with no concept of true theatrical criticism. At the bottom of the note was a little drawing of someone being stabbed in the back. Clovis James had the hand-written note framed and propped it up on his desk next to his typewriter in his office.

Three months after returning home from London, Peyton Chase stood at Idlewilde Airport, excitedly awaiting a flight from Paris. He was clutching a large bouquet of red roses, although Billy had mockingly teased him that it was so cliché.

A tall, exceptionally beautiful young woman with close-cropped black hair and sparkling emerald green eyes stood in front of the customs desk as the young officer thumbed through the pages in her French passport. He looked up at her, winked, and smiled as he stamped the book. She smiled coyly right back at him, lowering her eyes in an effort to look bashful.

"Welcome to America. Enjoy your stay, Miss…" and he glanced at the name in her passport once again, "… Alexis Morgan."

Author's Notes

"Books and doors are the same thing. You open them,
and you go through into another world."
Jeanette Winterson

The Night Witches actually were a true part of World War II history,
Google them. Fascinating story. Their subsequent revenge murders
following the war, however, are pure Hasbrouck fiction.

After reading about it and for the sheer fun of it, I gave Devon Stone,
my suave murderer, a condition that is called hyperthymesia...a condition
that hadn't been diagnosed until 2006. Obviously people may have had
this rare condition throughout the centuries, although no one realized that
it was an astonishing gift or, for that matter, a handicap. I Googled it. The
word "hyperthymesia" derives from the ancient Greek: *hyper-* (excessive) and
thymesis (remembering). It is so extraordinarily rare that only about 60 people
in the world have been diagnosed with this condition as of 2021. Amazing!

Murder on the Street of Years takes place, coincidentally, the same year that
another fictional character closely associated with MI6 came into being: *007*.
I certainly see definite similarities between that author, Ian Fleming,
and my character of Devon Stone. Although I seriously doubt that Fleming
ever committed murders, revenge or otherwise.

Acknowledgements

My deep love and admiration for my exceptionally gifted grandchildren inspired me to usurp their first and middle names to be used as characters in this book. I sincerely apologize to you, Jake, aka Hazzy. I had to make one of you boys a villain and you won (or lost) the coin-toss.

Needless to say, as good-looking as they all are, my grandchildren bear absolutely no resemblance, physical or behavioral, to their fictional counterparts. Well, with one exception. The real Peyton *loves* to fly and actually has a pilot's license.

| Devon Stone | Jacob Everett | Alexis Morgan | Peyton Chase |
| Hasbrouck | Hasbrouck | Hasbrouck | Hasbrouck |

I am sincerely grateful to so many of my friends who claimed to have read and enjoyed my books. The encouragement that they have given me to continue writing is overwhelming. I appreciate each and every one of them.

To say that I love our two sons, Gregory and Christopher, to the Nth degree is an understatement. I hope that they will forgive me for giving two of my characters personalities as far removed from theirs as could possibly be. As far as I know, neither one has ever committed a crime, major or minor.

Last but never least, the sharpest critic I have ever known is the one who shares my bed. My wife of 57 years, Gaylin Hasbrouck, has put up with my crazy shenanigans, writing or otherwise, with patience and with very few reprimands. Having been my best friend for the past 64 years helps tremendously. I love you more, dear heart. And thanks.

Printed in the United States
by Baker & Taylor Publisher Services